C000062750

Typeset in Adobe Garamond Pro

Software: Adobe InDesign®, Adobe Photoshop®

ISBN: 978-0-9560484-0-0

First Published November 2008 by Alberts Press

Alberts Press

135 Northview

Northumberland NE28 7PP

British Library Cataloguing In Publication Data

A Record of This Publication is available from the British Library

PANTO

Slim Palmer

Also available - written as Stiofan McAtinney:
OPERATION BRUTUS

I would like to thank the following for allowing this geriatric techie to participate in the Tyne Theatre and Opera House, Newcastle upon Tyne, pantomime season of 2007/8:
All the former staff, cast, crew and producers who include Brendan H, Maxie & Mitch, Tom S, Dags W, Davey L, Craig D, Simon P, Peter M, Ali Mc and last, but not least, Don I.
Without them this book would not have happened.
Thanks guys & galls - break a leg.

AUTHORS NOTE:

The world of theatre, like many professions, has its own language for various places and items. Listed below are just a few that you may find in the text:

FX	Effects / Special Effects. This may be lighting, sound, pyrotechnics or any mix.
LX	Lighting
OP	Opposite Prompt. Normally the right hand side of the stage as you look out to the auditorium.
PS / Prompt	Prompt Side. Normally the left hand side of the stage as you look out to the auditorium.
AJ	Adjustable Spanner.
Techie	Anyone who works backstage.
Twirly	A Dancer.
Hemp	Rope.
Grid	The area above the stage where the pulleys for the flying system are located.
Book	The marked-up script used by the prompter to cue the show.
Further theatre quirks may be found on the internet.	

Slim Palmer 2008

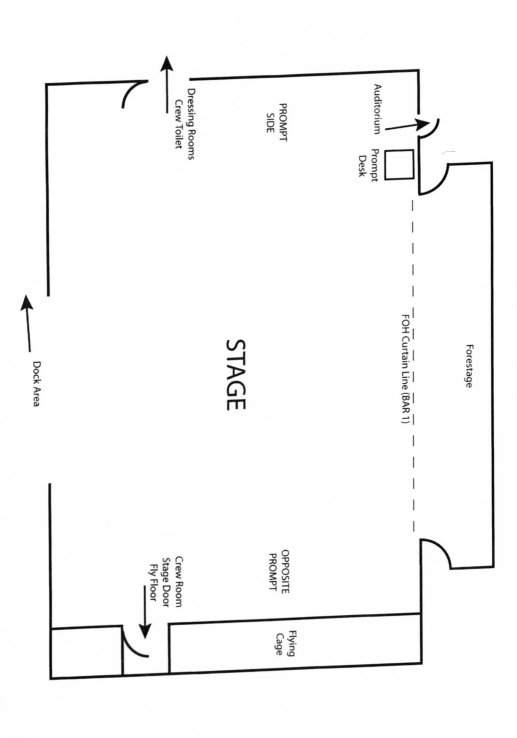

PROLOGUE

Subject: Panto script
From: Flynn Forbins <fforbins@theatresnet.com>
Date: 15 Aug 2007 07.57.46
To: Dan O'Leary <doleary1@theatresnet.com>

Dan,
Please find attached the first Act of the rough initial draft of the proposed panto. Let me know if this is ok so I may continue. Changes etc.
Thanks,
Flynn.

```
                    ALADDIN - PANTO


ACT I - SCENE 1 - THE MARKET PLACE IN OLD PEKING
   WITH TRADERS AND TOWNSPEOPLE. THE TOWNSPEOPLE
                CARRY SHOPPING BAGS.
   OPENING SONG / DANCE: 'Come to The Supermarket
                 In Old Peking'.


   ENTER TWANKEY IN A RICKSHAW. SHE STOPS TO TALK
                   TO ALADDIN.
            ENTER TWO POLICEMEN.
```

POLICEMEN:
Silence for a royal proclamation!

TANNOY-TYPE VOICE (off stage):
By order of his supreme majesty, Pak Po Duk,
Emperor of China!
The Princess Su Duk-oh will pass this way!
Any person found gazing upon her will be
executed. So be it!

ENTER PRINCESS AND SLOWLY CROSSES STAGE.
ALL TRADERS AND TOWNSPEOPLE FALL TO THEIR KNEES
OR BOW THEIR HEADS.
ALADDIN CREEPS AROUND THE RICKSHAW AND LOOKS AT
PRINCESS.

ALADDIN:
(AMAZED AT HER BEAUTY) Phwore!

THE TWO POLICEMEN SEE ALADDIN.
ALADDIN DASHES ACROSS STAGE FOLLOWED BY THE
TWO POLCEMEN BLOWING WHISTLES [BUSINESS: COULD
INCLUDE ALADDIN BEING CAPTURED BY POLICEMEN IN
HIS HIDING IN A LARGE ALI BABA BASKET - COMEDY
PATTER INCLUDING TIEING UP BASKET - WHEN IT IS
LIFTED THE BOTTOM FALLS OUT AND HE ESCAPES].

ACT I - SCENE 2: ABANAZER'S DEEP AND DARK LAIR.
ABANAZER APPEARS AND RUBS HIS HANDS TOGETHER.

ABANAZER:

Come to me Oh Genie of the Ring. I command you!

GENIE OF THE RING APPEARS.

GENIE OF THE RING:

You summon me Oh great master?

ABANAZER:

I would have you tell me how I may acquire the
lamp that I so greatly desire?

GENIE OF THE RING:

You must seek a boy in a far off land. He alone
can get what you desire.

ABANAZER:

Which boy! Where?

GENIE OF THE LAMP:

In far off China there lives a boy called
Aladdin.

ABANAZER:

I command you: Take me to this boy!

ABANAZER AND GENIE DISAPPEAR.

ACT I - SCENE 3: WIDOW TWANKEY'S LAUNDRY.

WISHEE WASHEE ENTERS WITH A BIG PILE OF DIRTY
CLOTHES AND GOES TOWARDS A LARGE LAUNDRY SKIP -
HE TAKES A DETOUR DOWNSTAGE AND ALMOST LOSES THE
CLOTHES INTO THE AUDIENCE.

WISHEY:
Oh! Hello kids. (Audience response).
(LOUDER) Hello Kids! (Audience response).
I'm Wishey Washee and this is my mum's
laundrette. She's out shopping - as usual - so I
have to do some of the work for my pocket money.
Look what I found in one of the laundry baskets.
(TAKES BAG FROM TOP OF LAUNDRY PILE)
Sweets. I'll never eat them all so who likes
sweets? (Audience response)

(THROWS SWEETS TO AUDIENCE).

Well I can't spend all day talking to you I have
to get this lot (INDICATES CLOTHES PILE) into
the basket.

HE STAGGERS TO THE SKIP AND DUMPS THE LAUNDRY
INTO IT (LID UP) AND HALF FALLS IN AFTER IT.

TWANKY ENTERS WITH BULGING SHOPPING BAGS.

TWANKEY:

Yoo-hoo! Wishey! I'm home!

WISHEY STANDS UP - HE HAS A SET OF BLOOMERS ON
HIS HEAD.

WISHEY:

(muffled voice) Hello mum. Been shopping?

TWANKEY STARES AT WISHEY FOR A MOMENT THEN
SEARCHES HER SHOPPING.

TWANKEY:

I knew I'd forgotten something.

WISHEY QUICKLY REMOVES THE BLOOMERS FROM HIS
HEAD AND DROPS THEM IN THE SKIP.

WISHEY:

Looks like you bought everything in town.

TWANKEY:

I got some amazing bargains. Matalan (OR OTHER
STORE) had fifty percent off everything. Look.

SHE PULLS THE LEFT HALF A DRESS (ON A HANGER)
FROM A CARRIER BAG.

WISHEE:

I suppose you're spent up? I was hoping for my
pocket money as there's a new game for the Why-
Aye I wanted to get.

TWANKEY:

Weeee

WISHEY:

Upstairs and second door on the left.

TWANKEY:

No, no. It's said Wee.

WISHEY PONDERS FOR A BEAT OR TWO AND PULLS FROM THE SKIP AN EMPTY SOAP POWDER BOX.

WHISHEY:

I bet you forgot to buy more so… ap?

ALADDIN (OFFSTAGE):

Quick… quick!

ALADDIN RUNS ON STAGE.

ALADDIN:

Quick. Hide me the coppers are chasing me!

WISHEY INDICATES THE SKIP AND ALADDIN JUMPS IN PULLING THE LID CLOSED. WISHEY SITS ON THE SKIP.

ENTER POLICEMEN WITH TRUNCHEONS DRAWN.

POLICEMAN PING:

You sure he ran in here, Officer Pong?

POLICEMAN PONG:
I am, Officer Ping.

PING:
Widow Twankey we shall have to search your
location.

TWANKEY SMILES AND HOLDS UP HER ARMS AS IF
WANTING TO BE FRISKED.

TWANKEY:
Ooh! Best offer I've had all day.

PONG:
No, no. The premises. Your Aladdin dared to look
at the Princess Su Duk-oh and we have to arrest
him. He'll get ASBO'd for this.

(PONG STARTS TO SEARCH)

WISHEY:
I though looking at the Princess meant you got
your head chopped off?

PING:
That's what he said. ASBO'd. A Slight Bend
Over and then… (MAKES CHOPPING MOTION WITH HIS
TRUNCHEON).

PONG APPROACHES LAUNDRY SKIP AND TRIES TO LIFT
LID. WISHEY STAYS SEATED.

PONG:

Only place left to look.

WHISHEY:

Oh, he can't be in here.

PONG:

Oh yes, he can.

WHISHEY (to audience):

Oh no, he can't.

PING (to audience):

Oh yes, he can.

WHISHEY:

Oh no, he can't.

PING AND PONG LIFT THE STILL SEATED WISHEY FROM
THE SKIP AND PLACE HIM ON STAGE.
PING OPENS THE LID AND DUCKS DOWN BEHIND IT.

PING:

Phwaar! Worra pong!

PING SLAMS LID SHUT.

PONG:

Yes I am actually. Named after my great uncle.

PING:

No, no. The smell in there is awful. Who are you
doing washing for?

WHISHEY TURNS SKIP 180 DEGREES TO REVEAL
(FOOTBALL CLUB) LOGO.

WISHEY:

That'll be the (football team) underpants.

PONG:

Sorry to have bothered you Widow Twankey. Come
on Ping I bet he ducked up that back lane.

PING & PONG EXIT.

WISHEY GOES TO THE SKIP AND LIFTS THE LID.
ALADDIN ARISES FROM THE SKIP WITH A GIANT
CLOTHES PEG ON HIS NOSE.

ALADDIN:

(Speaking through nose) Have they gone?

TWANKEY PULLS CLOTHES PEG FROM HIS NOSE.

TWANKEY:

The shame… the shame…

ENTER ABANAZER

ABANAZER:

Not shame madam. Actually it is pronounced
shaman. I greet you as a relative. (HE MAKES A
GREAT FLOURISH).

TWANKEY:

Ooh!... Relative to what?

ABANAZER:

I am your long-lost brother-in-law, Abanazer. I
have been overseas for many years and, hearing
of your widow-hood, I am here to assist you with
my two nephews.

WISHEY:

Does this mean we get pocket money?

ALADDIN STEPS FROM THE SKIP AND JOINS WISHEY.
THEY BOTH HOLD OUT THEIR HANDS.

TWANKEY:

I don't think my husband ever mentioned someone
called 'ave Abanana?

ABANAZER:

Abanazer!

WISHEY AND ALADDIN STEP FURTHER FORWARD. THEY
BOTH STILL HOLD OUT THEIR HANDS.

TWANKEY:

Don't be greedy boys. I'm sure he hasn't come

all this way just to give you pocket money. Have you Mister 'ave a nosey?

ABANAZER:

Ab-a-nazer!

TWANKEY FLIRTS WITH ABANAZER.

TWANKEY:

You are rather handsome and… tall… and… rich?

ABANAZER:

I am rich in many ways madam. And, with the help of Aladdin, I shall be richer still.

TWANKEY:

Ooh…!

ABANAZER REACHES INTO HIS ROBES AND PULLS OUT A PURSE.

ABANAZER:

I am, of course, willing to pay for Aladdin's help in a certain quest that I have.

TWANKEY FLUTTERS AROUND ABANAZER TAKING THE PURSE AS SHE DOES SO. SHE OPENS IT AND LOOKS INSIDE.

TWANKEY:

(aside) An hour on a sunbed; forty quid. Dinner at the Gosforth Park (top hotel); hundred and

twenty quid. Aladdin out of the way… Ooh…! Less
. . . . Price. (to Abanazer) He'll do it! . . . .
. . . .
. . . . ACT I - SCENE 4: A MOUNTAIN RAVINE . . . . . .
. . . .
ENTER ABANAZER FOLLOWED BY ALADDIN. THEY ARE
. . . . FIGHTING AGAINST A STRONG WIND. . . . .

ALADDIN:

(Whinging) Are we there yet?

ABANAZER:

(Frustrated) Aagh! Almost.

ALADDIN:

You never said it would be this flipping cold!

ABANAZER:

Will you stop complaining!

PAUSE.

ALADDIN:

(Whinging) Are we there yet?

THEY APPROACH A LARGE STONE WHICH COVERS A CAVE.

ABANAZER:

This is the place.

ALADDIN:
What? A big rock?

ABANAZER:
That which we seek is behind the rock.

ALADDIN: (TAKES COMPASS FROM TROUSERS)
It sits north.

ABANAZER:
It does?

ALADDIN:
We have to move this to see what is behind it?

ABANAZER:
... or make it fall away.

ALADDIN:
I don't think the economy could stand that a
second time.

ABANAZER:
What?

ALADDIN:
A second collapse of the Northern Rock.

ABANAZER:
(frustrated) Boy! I shall use magic to move the
rock!

ALADDIN:

That's what Richard Branston said.

ABANAZER:

With one phrase I shall move this stone to
reveal the cave behind it!

ALADDIN:

Not that old hackneyed thing about Open Sesame?

ABANAZER:

(affronted) How do you know of this?

ALADDIN:

Wishey worked in the Burger King bun section for
a while.

ABANAZER FACES THE ROCK AND SHOOTS HIS HANDS
TOWARDS IT.

ABANAZER:

Open Sesame!

ALADDIN:

Sooo last century…

ABANAZER:

If you know better then you tell me boy!

ALADDIN LEANS INTO ABANAZER AND WHISPERS IN HIS
EAR.

ABANAZER:
You're sure?

ALADDIN NODS.
ABANAZER FACES THE ROCK AND SHOOTS HIS HANDS
TOWARDS IT.

ABANAZER:
123 (to follow)

THE ROCK SLOWLY MOVES TO THE SIDE TO REVEAL A
CAVE ENTRANCE.
ALADDIN CUPS HIS HANDS TO HIS MOUTH AND SHOUTS
INTO CAVE.

ALADDIN:
Yoo-hoo… Mister Bin Laden…?

ABANAZER:
Wrong!... This is the entrance to an object that
I seek. The lamp that I told you of. Descend the
stairs and we shall be rich when you return.

ALADDIN STICK HIS HEAD THROUGH THE CAVE ENTANCE
AND THEN TURNS TO ABANAZER

ALADDIN:
Looks a bit spooky to me… And dark.

ABANAZER:
Just go down the stairs. It will get lighter in the cave. Once you are there look for a lamp – do not touch anything else. Nothing but the lamp!

ALADDIN MAKES TO CROSS THE CAVE THREASHOLD BUT PAUSES FOR A MOMENT.

ALADDIN:
Just the lamp?

ABANAZER:
Just the lamp.

ALADDIN ENTERS THE CAVE ENTRANCE.

ALADDIN:
Aladdin is in the cave.

ABANAZER:
Ha! Ha! Soon my plans will all come together! The stupid boy will get me the lamp and I shall rule all before me! Ha! Ha! Ha!

ALADDIN JUMPS OUT OF THE CAVE.

ALADDIN:

A lad out the cave.

ABANAZER:

Do not test me boy! Go and get the lamp!

ALADDIN:

It's really dark down there. There's spiders and
bats and ghoulies and ghosties and things that
might go bump. I need a light.

ABANAZER THROWS UP HIS HANDS IN FRUSTRATION.

ABANAZER:

Take this. (REMOVES RING FROM FINGER AND PASSES
IT TO ALADDIN) It will give a small glow when
you enter the darkness. It should be enough.
Now get me the lamp!

ALADDIN ENTERS THE CAVE.

ALADDIN:

It's a bit dark down here…

ABANAZER: (into cave)

Hold the ring in front of you. It will help.
Does it glow?

ALADDIN:

It's glowing.

ABANAZER: (to audience)
At last! At last! (LAUGHS)

ACT I - SCENE 5: THE CAVE

ALADDIN DESCENDS THE STAIRS INTO THE DARK CAVE.
THE RING IS HIS ONLY ILLUMINATION (IRIS DOWN F/
SPOT).

ALADDIN
It's a bit spooky down here.

SKELETON TURNS HEAD TO LOOK AT HIM. AS HE
ADVANCES THOUGH CAVE MORE SKELETONS TURN TO
LOOK.

ALADDIN (to audience)
Ever get the feeling you're not alone?
Did you see anything?

SKELETONS ADVANCE ON ALADDIN

ALADDIN
Where?

AUDIENCE REACTION - PLAY ON REACTION UNTIL
EVENTUALLY BUMP INTO SKELETON.

ALADDIN

Whoar! You're a… bones… thingy… Skeleton!

SKELETONS SURROUND ALADDIN, PULL AT HIM AND THEN
START DANCING (poss Techno?) ALADDIN HIDES.

AT END OF DANCE SKELETONS ADVANCE ON ALADDIN.
ALADDIN (FRIGHTENED) ASKS AUDIENCE:

ALADDIN (TO AUDIENCE)
Do you think if I rubbed the ring it would make
it brighter and they would go away?

ALADDIN RUBS RING.
GENIE APPEARS AND SKELETONS SHY BACK AND EXIT.

*** STUFF HERE WITH LAMP GENIE, TREASURE DANCERS
ETC...

. . . .
. . . .
. . . .
. . . . END ACT I . . . .
. . . .
. . . .

ACT II - SCENE 1: WIDOW TWANKEY'S LAUNDRY

. . . .

ACT II - SCENE 2: A STREET IN PEKING

• •

ACT II - SCENE 3: ALADDIN'S PALACE

• •

ACT II - SCENE 4: NEW LAMPS FOR OLD

• •

ACT II - SCENE 5: THE FLYING CARPET

• •

ACT II - SCENE 6: ABANAZAR'S RETREAT

• •

ACT II - SCENE 6: THE GRAND FINALE

PANTO

NOVEMBER

Despite the fact that the holiday rep had said that Gran Canaria's *Puerto Rico* resort was "a place of twos: two shopping centres, two ports and too many fucking steps to the beach", Rob had booked a fortnight, even though he didn't do shopping, sailing or sand. He was now sitting on the terrace of his apartment overlooking the harbour that the ferries used, as he had been all morning since the sun rose at about six am. As it was rising he'd breakfasted on the sweetest, juiciest slice of local melon he had ever tasted, and now, at eight thirty, he was about to open his first can of Dorada beer, the local brew, and to light up his first six and a half inch *Alvaro Elegantes* grand corona of the day – a bargain at eighteen Euros for twenty-five – to fill the surrounding air with the aromatic smell of Sumatran and Javanese tobacco.

The Canaries had not been his first thought when he decided to take an early winter break; Greece was his first choice, Spain was second. However, the price with the single person supplement had been right. The two thousand pounds that he had won on the lottery offered his last chance to relax before he had to settle into life on the State back home in the UK.

At fifty-one there was no chance of being able to get back into theatre. He stretched his six foot three frame to its full extent on the recliner, to take advantage of the ever increasing heat from the sun and, patting his gut, kicked off his flip-flops. He was exactly eleven stone. Everyone had said that when he had to quit physical work that he would pile on the pounds; they had been wrong. In the theatre he had been twelve stone of muscle. Eleven was good even though the heaviest thing he had lifted for years had been a full pint glass.

'Jeez. Theatre. That had been good,' he said to himself and then, as he had many times before, contemplated what had happened to him in the last twelve years.

That was two's as well: two marriages, two divorces, two kids, two jobs.

It had all gone tits up when he'd badly dislocated his shoulder down at the Liverpool Empire seven years ago. End of touring, end of theatre and physio for a year. That was the year, no two years, in which he had gone to college to re-train as a graphic designer – or as it said on the course paper, 'Multimedia Design'.

And he'd been good at it. With no previous knowledge of computers or the associated software, as a mature student he had picked it up as he would pick up a stage weight. It had just come to him naturally. Before he knew it he was asked to teach night-classes and then, on graduation, had been taken on as a lecturer. That was when he'd started the design company.

Clients had been so easy to find. The Health Service, local councils, big, middling, local and international clients. Marriage. Second divorce – the hours were not conducive to wives – and finally going bust.

The two thousand had been a god-send. He finished the Dorada and crushed the can.

A knock at the door.

'Hola!' he replied.

The door opened and the daily maid poked her head around it; 'I do now?' she enquired.

'Si,' replied Rob, 'Gracias.'

For the ten days he been there, right on cue at, more or less, nine o'clock, the maid had knocked at his door to ask the same question.

He had guessed that his was the first room on the list as when asking how many places she had to clean – in broken Spanish – she had showed him a list of twelve apartment numbers.

'Tres horas I do' she had explained.

Fifteen minutes an apartment wasn't bad going, seeing as how she not only mopped all of the rooms' marble floors, made up the bed and, as a bonus, washed any dishes that were left over from the night before.

Rob went back to pondering his predicament.

Twenty minutes later he made a decision. Walk up the *Calle Roque del Este* to the supermercado and get some more Doradas, water and some *queso, jamon y pan*. He just fancied a cheese and ham toasted sandwich for a late lunch. If they had any of those large, locally grown tomatoes he would get some of those as well. Delicious didn't come into it. You could taste the sun in that fruit.

Afterwards he would walk the mile or so down the hill to the town centre "hopping Centre" – he had noticed on his first night that the 'S' on the prominent illuminated sign was missing – and have another look into the myriad of shops to see if there were any bargains apart from booze and cigars. It was a bit of a nuisance that the Canaries were part of Spain but were excluded from the European Union duty free quotas.

Half way across the *Avenida de la Gomera*, outside the centre, his mobile phone rang and he answered it with 'Hang on!' as he narrowly missed being run over by one of the green and black taxi cabs that scurried about taking tourists back up the hills to their apartments. Safely on the pavement he put the phone to his ear. 'Hello?'

'Rob?'

'Yeah.'

'Noodles…'

'Hello, mate; long time no hear.'

'I'm in Newcastle so I thought I'd give you a buzz to see if you fancied going for a pint… or three?'

'Sorry mate, no can do…'

'Oh?'

'I'm a bit far away at the moment.'

Ah, right. Somewhere nice?'

Rob paused for a moment and then with a grin said, 'Isle of Dogs.'

'Jeez… What you got – a job at Canary Wharf?'

'Not that dog island; the other one.'

'The other one?'

'Islas de Canaria.'

'Blimey, alright for some. You holidaying or working?'

'Trying to sort my life out…' Rob muttered, and then, 'holiday.'

'When are you back?'

'Three or four days. Why?'

'Like I said; go for a pint or three with some of the old crowd and maybe do a bit of work later on this year.'

'What sort of work?'

'What do you think?'

'You mean… theatre?'

'Might be…' replied Noodles conspiratorially.

The dull thump of the undercarriage locking into place woke Rob from his dream and the first thing he saw was the shorts covered backside of a large woman bending over in the aisle to put her shoes back on.

Sitting up straight and twisting the crick out of his neck he observed the rest of the passengers on the aircraft.

It never ceased to amaze him that half or more of the unseasoned travellers wore their holiday clothes when re-entering Britain – did they not realise that it might be twenty-seven degrees three thousand miles away but probably minus two and sleeting on their return – especially in early November?

The young couple to his left, in the window and centre seats, were holding hands. The girl's knuckles were white with anticipation.

'Far to go?' asked the male teenager.

'Huh?'

'When we land. Have you got far to go home?'

'No,' replied Rob, 'not far.'

The cabin lights dimmed for the night-time landing and the girl gave a sharp intake of breath. Her knuckles became whiter and the boy's fingers redder.

'We're from Sunderland. Her dad's picking us up.'

Rob nodded.

The aircraft wheels bumped the tarmac and the brakes were applied.

The girl gave a slight whimper.

'She doesn't fly well' stated the youth, by way of explanation.

Rob just nodded again.

'Welcome to Newcastle,' said a clipped female voice over the loudspeaker system. 'We hope you enjoyed your holiday with Pack Tours and that you will travel with us again? The temperature outside is six degrees and there is a slight drizzle. Please have your passports ready for immigration and remain seated until the aircraft comes to a full stop. Again, thank you for flying with Pack Tours.'

'It's hardly likely to come to a comma, is it?' suggested the youth by way of a joke.

'I doubt it,' agreed Rob.

As soon as the aircraft pulled up, people were on their feet and collecting bags and assorted possessions from the overhead lockers. Rob just sat and waited even though he could see that the girl was twitching to get out of her seat.

'Don't see any point in rushing,' he remarked, 'they haven't even got the exit stairs in place yet.'

The "slight drizzle" proved to be an almost horizontal downpour and felt freezing as Rob walked to the terminal building. He was glad of the blouson fleece jacket and denim jeans that he had worn for the flight, even though some of the other travellers had given him an old fashioned look as he had sat in the Canaries airport waiting for his rearranged transport – it had been relatively simple to change his flight from Gatwick to Newcastle by seeing the apartment complex holiday rep.

Passport control was a couple of bored looking women in uniform who stared at the open pages, stared at him and then, passing back the passport, waved him through to the baggage collection area.

'Just knowing my luck it'll be last off,' thought Rob referring to his suitcase.

The carousel lurched into life as he and his fellow travellers strained to watch the cavernous hole out of which the luggage would soon spew. The carousel stopped again, to an audible and frustrated sigh from those assembled. Seconds later it restarted and luggage started to fall from the hole. Rob's case was first.

'Result!' he grinned, hoping that none of the four bottles of "103" brandy and two hundred cigars had been damaged. Bugger the regulations.

The black cab pulled up on the rain drenched road under the street light, opposite the house, as instructed. The rain had now stopped.

'Twelve quid mate,' said the driver.

Rob fumbled through his wallet separating euros from pound notes and pulled out a twenty, passing it through the sliding window. 'Call it fifteen.'

'Cheers,' answered the driver passing back a five pound note.

As the cab pulled away Rob stood under the streetlight and observed the mid-terraced house. It was as he remembered it.

It had been his mother's place until her death a couple of years ago. This house and a few pieces of gold jewellery, together with a thousand pound "funeral fund" were all that she had left to Rob. Luckily, ex-wife number two had been out of the way for about six months when his mother had died, or else all this would have been part of the settlement as well.

He crossed the road and walked up the short path, keys in hand.

On closing the front door he noticed a small envelope pinned to the lobby door, it read *Robert*, in a copperplate hand.

Carrying his case up the short passage he let himself into the rear living room and noticed it was warm.

'Good on you, Aunty Lil,' he noted before depositing his luggage and flopping down on the large two-seater sofa to read the note.

Robert,

Glad to hear you are paying us a visit for Xmas.

I have put on the heating and made up a bed for you in your old room.

There is some milk and bread in the fridge, a couple of ready meals in the freezer and I've left some tea bags and some sugar.

Love,

Aunty Lil.

Rob grinned at the thought of the next door neighbour still being "Aunty Lil" after all this time. She wasn't a blood relative but had insisted that she be called "Aunty" when the family had moved in when Rob was about nine or ten years old. She would be in her eighties by now.

Rob glanced at his new Canarian watch – he'd bartered a hundred euros off the price that the trader had wanted for it. Eleven thirty; too late to give her a knock.

After a large brandy and a cigar he went to bed.

Rob opened his eyes slowly and looked at his wrist; he had slept for twelve hours – either that or the new watch was wrong. He glanced at the bedside clock, sitting in a fine patina of dust, which he had wound up before putting his head down the previous night. Nine-thirty.

'Typical,' he observed, bemoaning the fact that any wristwatch he had ever owned had either gained or lost time when he wore them. After a shower and some fresh clothes he made some tea and toast and rang the number that he had for Lil – even though she was just a wall away.

'Hello?' said a frail voice after the sixth or seventh ring.

'Hi, Aunty Lil, it's Rob.'

'Robert. I heard you rattling around earlier. Everything all right?'

'Yes, fine. Thanks for the bits 'n' pieces and the heating.'

'Oh it was nothing. When will I see you?'

'Give me time to finish my tea and I'll give you a knock.'

'Lovely.' She rang off.

Rob dialled Noodles' number, stored from their conversation four days earlier.

'Noodles,' came the curt answer.

'Hi, it's Rob.'

'Rob! Can I ring you back? I'm up to my ears in hemp at the moment.'

'The rope kind I hope?' Rob answered with a grin.

'There's another kind?' he replied with a chuckle, 'ring you back in half an hour.' With that, the line went dead.

He did his duty by seeing his next door neighbour, presenting her with a bottle of brandy to the predictable response, 'That'll go well on the Christmas pud.' He promised the old lady that he would keep popping in and that finally, he would take her to visit the theatre where he used to work.

"You've been promising me for years, Robert,' she had chided.

'I promise,' he'd insisted, 'I'll take you to the theatre.'

Rob returned to the settee to await Noodles' call.

Noodles' call came an hour later.

After the pleasantries of asking how the holiday had gone and was the flight back good, Noodles asked, 'What are you doing at lunchtime?'

'Hadn't thought about it. Why?'

'Pint?'

'Yeah, okay, where?'

'I'm down at the theatre so how about the place a couple of doors up?'

'*Billy's* you mean?'

'Hah! *Billy's* is long gone. When's the last time you were up here?'

Rob had to think hard. 'About seven years ago. Came to see Mum.'

'There's a heck of a lot changed since then. See you in *The Bodger* at one?'

'*The Bodger*? Okay, one o'clock.'

The taxi dropped Rob off opposite the theatre and he stood and looked at the building that had been his place of work for a lot of years, now in the past.

It still appeared the same. A blue and gold façade and a glass canopy that was still in need of a good clean due to pigeon droppings and algae, rising to an Italianate-style frontage.

He noticed that it had been given a new name. Instead of *The Royal Theatre & Opera House* it was now sponsored, he presumed, by the local newspaper and was inelegantly now called *The Herald Royal Theatre*.

Looking towards the foyer entrance he noticed a sign across the glass panel of all the doors: "A REAG Venue".

'Well fuck my old steelies,' he exclaimed, 'the bastards actually got hold of the place.' He referred to a time when he had fought with the other stage and lighting technicians to try and prevent the theatre being taken over by a corporation and turned into a bingo hall. 'Eyes fucking down.'

'Heads up!' exclaimed a voice just to his right and behind him.

Rob's instant reaction was to place his arms across his head and duck down, the term being used on stage when something had been dropped from above, but just stopped himself.

'Glad to see you haven't entirely lost it,' said the man now standing before Rob.

Noodles looked almost the same as he had fifteen or more years ago, albeit he had put on some weight – gone from about twelve stone to about fifteen. And the ginger-blond hair, that many woman would have died for, had receded slightly, but it was still the same shoulder length. He pulled up his five foot ten frame and thrust out a meaty hand to Rob.

As they shook hands Rob wondered if he still lived up to his nickname and existed on a diet of Chinese food.

Before he could ask the question Noodles said, 'C'mon I'll buy you a pint.' He nodded up the street to where a green-fronted bar with etched-windowed stood, bearing the legend *Bodgers* over the double doors.

'It used to be something else, didn't it?' asked Rob, looking up at the sign as they entered the pub.

'Dirty Duck,' was Noodles reply, 'full of old men, spit, sawdust, whippets, betting slips and Brown Ale.'

The place had changed – drastically. The floors were now varnished boards instead of lumpy linoleum; the bar had been lengthened to run down what appeared to be the entire right side of the room and there were now booths around the walls and long wooden tables towards the rear. Even the ceiling was different. Rob seemed to remember it being lower and acoustically tiled – now it was vaulted and had a domed, stained glass sky-light.

They sidled up to the empty bar.

'The usual "Nigerian Lager"?' asked Noodles.

Rob nodded as he took in the rest of the décor, which seemed to be aimed at the real ale drinkers.

Whilst the pints settled he noticed a bar menu and took a quick glance at it. Not bad prices for a city centre pub.

'The steak 'n' ale pie's excellent,' recommended Noodles. 'Should we join the rest?' He passed across the Guinness.

'Rest. What rest?' Rob asked, as he flicked the overflowing froth from his fingers to the floor.

Noodles just grinned and led the way to the rear of the pub, which was half hidden behind a divider that hid an ATM machine. Six heads turned at once from the long table behind it.

The grinning faces stopped Rob in his tracks and he almost dropped his pint.

'Slap me grummets and fly me out on a truss!' he exclaimed, 'What the fuck are you lot doing here?' he smiled.

Sitting around the table were some of Rob's old techie crew from when he'd been stage manager at the theatre next door, and a couple of possible strangers – one of them looking very young – sitting at the next table but apparently part of Noodles' company, because they smiled at him.

Foz, Rob's former 'second', was still his tall, rangy self apart from the absence of the flowing curls that used to end halfway down his back – even when worn in a ponytail. They'd been trimmed to collar length and had a fleck of grey at the temples. The last Rob had heard of him he was employed at a garage doing grease-monkey work.

Tam, a Scot of mixed parentage (his mother being Spanish), didn't look any different from the last time Rob had seen him. Pale olive skin, two day stubble and a full head of black hair trimmed to his neck. He had been off the radar – with regard to theatre work – when Rob had last enquired.

Dickie, well educated and slightly camp, looked up from the book that he still seemed permanently to have his nose in, pulled at the end of his goatee and winked a greeting as he wiped his hand over the receded stubble of his hairline. His stint over the past few years as Rob understood it, teaching the craft of stage management at a local collage, seemed to have left him more determined, Rob thought, to go his own way. Then again Dickie had always been his own person.

Tom was the former stage door keeper, very camp – he played on it and let everyone know – and Stevie was one of the best flymen in the business.

It was Stevie who stood out the most. He was wearing a suit.

'Job interview or court appearance?' Rob grinned, 'nice bit of schmutter.' He leant over the table to feel the lapel of the suit.

'Nah! had to get a proper effin job after our lass had two more kids, the former flyman grinned. 'Call centre. Good money though.'

'How're you doing Tom? Blimey, I thought you'd be well retired by now!'

'Many a good tune played on an old fiddle,' he smiled back, raising his glass.

'Aye, an' we know all aboot yer fiddling,' grinned Tam.

'Jeez guys! It's good to see you all.' Rob raised his glass and saluted them before taking a deep drink.

It was not long before they got to reminiscing about the "old days" and stories of pseudo-heroics, drunken nights and what absolute bastards some shows had been. Finally, several pints later, Noodles tapped an empty glass on the table for silence.

'The reason I asked you all here...' he paused, '... is to pull me out of the shit.'

All faces were attentive.

'The REAG bunch next door promised that I would have a team of five crew for the show that I'm putting in over Christmas...'

'Panto,' stated Dickie.

Noodles nodded and continued: '... but I was told the other day that they had changed their policy and now I'm only getting one: the LX guy, Pendry.'

'Y' no seriously considerin'...?' he left the words unspoken but indicated the gathered company with an outstretched palm.

'I am,' was the reply. 'I need someone to second me, two wingmen a side and someone on props. Tom's already agreed to do the follow spot and part-time stage door.'

'What's the matter with the local crew; surely there must be some?' asked Stevie.

'Nope. All taken. There's a big Panto going in down the road'. There were two major theatres in the town, 'and the Haymarket has got the usual Christmas Show...'

'Ah, Art!' Rob grinned, flicking his fingers in the air to imitate quote marks.

There was general laughter around the table.

'What about out of town guys?' asked Foz.

Noodles shook his head, 'All working.'

There was a pause whilst everyone took in what had been said.

'It's been seven years since I did any theatre stuff, Noodles. Christ, the heaviest thing I've lifted is the ex. On and off – several times,' stated Rob.

'Y' mean three?' grinned Tam.

'No way I can do it,' interjected Stevie, 'the wife'd kill us and I couldn't get the effin time off work.' He swallowed the last of his lager with a gulp and headed to the bar for a re-fill.

'Three hundred quid a week,' stated Noodles by way of an incentive.

'Top line o' bottom?' asked Tam, his eyes glinting slightly at the mention of money and the possibility of not having to pay income tax.

'Cash.'

This news was met by several smiles.

'When's the start date?' asked Dickie, 'I've seen the flyer for the shows but when's the get in; fit up?'

Noodles nodded. 'Shows start on the Friday. Just one – which we're treating as a public dress; we would start on the Sunday previous to get the stuff through the doors. Fit up Monday and Tuesday; tech Wednesday; dress Thursday… according to plans.'

'Mice and men' mumbled Foz, just before emptying his glass.

Rob caught the aside and a smile flitted across his face because he knew full well that things never went to plan, or to put it in theatre parlance, "shit happens".

'My being out of it for so long - and not being in town; two questions?'

'Rob?'

'What's the show and who's in it?'

Before Noodles could reply to the question Stevie returned from the bar with a tray full of drinks. They were duly passed around. 'Sorry Guys, but I've got to get back to effin work. Sorry Noodles but … y'know…'

'Thanks for coming Stevie. Have a good 'un.' They shook hands and the former flyman tipped a wave as he left the pub.

'See y' Stevie!' was the chorused farewell.

'To answer Rob,' replied Noodles, 'it's Aladdin. It's all local talent. We've got the comedy duo Bigg 'n' Liddle as Ping and Pong; Aladdin is the local TV news announcer, Lynne Magee; Washee is another stand-up cum muso, Dan O'Leary…'

'Twankey?' asked Dickie.

'Jimmy Wands.'

'Known and loved in the community.' was the chorus this time, to quote the actor's self-promotional phrase.

'And of course Abanazer is that all time favourite – Frank "I really am nasty" Gartiner.'

The chorus was a loud "Boo!" followed by laughter.

'Emperor and Princess are locals as well. Twirlies are all local girls and a stage school are supplying three sets of babes,' continued Noodles.

'So a *Geordie* panto,' observed Dickie.

'That's the plan. ' He paused, and then added, 'Any thoughts?'

'I'm in,' this was from Dickie.

'Aye, in,' was Tam's acceptance.

'Count me in,' was Foz's response.

They all turned to look at Rob after a second or two.

'Rob?' asked Noodles.

'Seven years guys…' he spread his hands and grimaced.

'Bollocks!' exclaimed Tam, 'c'mon man: it'll be a bit o' fun.'

'Ahh… fuck it. Count me in.'

'Then let me introduce …' said Noodles, turning to the two strangers, who up until this point had not joined in the revelries, 'Sam.' Sam was a girl in her early twenties with short, thick, mousy hair. 'Sam's to be on the book. And this is Simmy, who was going to be our second on flys but has just been promoted to first.' Simmy was taller, with bleached blond hair that had a purple stripe running down the side parting. The two girls flipped a wave and smiled.

In the Gods bar, at the top of the theatre, the outside illumination from a sodium street light filtered through the window and ethereal blue lights played across the marble topped bar and skimmed the dusty carpet.

'I see that everyone is present mama should I ask for order?'

'If you would be so kind, Bertie.'

'I say… I say… ahem. Could we have a semblance of order as mama… erm… Her Ladyship… would like a few words.'

The lights arranged themselves, from mere wisps to globes of intense blue light, into a semi-circle around two others of similar intensity.

'Good evening ladies and gentlemen.'

'Evening Your Ladyship.'

'The time is almost upon us, once again, to walk the theatre. Christmas Eve has traditionally been our time. This year there is an exception.'

There was a slight hubbub from those assembled.

'Quiet please' instructed Bertie.

'The exception being,' continued the ethereal light, *'that there is nothing on in the theatre. It is dark. Since the takeover by these REAG people there is no longer a night watchman. We may, therefore, assume our former earthly guises as we walk – something that has not happened these past six years.'*

A cheer went up from the assembled company.

Rob woke, sprawled across the settee, with a half eaten donner kebab on his chest. For an iota he thought he'd been eviscerated.

His mouth felt as if a family of badgers had camped in it overnight.

'Tea, I need tea,' was his immediate thought.

Holding together, as best he could, last nights supper, he folded what was left of the meat, pitta bread, salad and salsa back into the polystyrene carton and deposited it into the kitchen flip-top bin, spilling only a slash of the red salsa mix onto the quarry-tiled floor.

As he waited for the kettle to boil he wiped the spill with a dishrag and mulled over the events of the previous evening. He had a nagging doubt that perhaps he had accepted too readily.

His mobile phone rang.

'Mornin'!' said a voice on the other end.

'Yeah?' Rob admitted, without enthusiasm.

'I bet you don't even have a hangover, you bastard.'

Rob grinned. 'Nope. Don't do those. How're you, Noodles?'

'Hung over, but ready for the meet 'n 'greet at the rehearsal rooms.'

Rob suddenly remembered the conversation he and Noodles had outside the Bodger, when they'd retired for a cigarette. He had to do an extra two weeks prior to the get-in with the cast at … Christ he couldn't remember.

'Yeah… erm… one o'clock we said.'

'You remembered.'

'Hnnn.' More by luck than good fortune.

Noodles then pulled him out of his predicament: 'One o'clock. Jesmond Church Hall. Sheesh, you even wrote it down.'

'Yeah, so I did,' he admitted, hurriedly searching through his pockets, 'see you there.'

'Yup'

The line went dead as the kettle clicked off, water boiled.

After two cups of tea, a slice of toast and three cigarettes, Rob decided to go and hunt out his theatre gear. He knew exactly where it was in the attic; inside the old pirate chest that had once starred in "Pirates of Penzance". It had been discarded at the end of the run and he had "acquired" it. Inside it would be his Maglite, Leatherman multitool, an AJ wrench, heavy gloves and, last but not least, his steel-toe-capped boots – together with other detritus of his past life.

'I haven't owned anything black for years,' he admitted out loud. 'I need to go shopping.'

Deciding against a cab to get to the rehearsals – what was left of his two grand was not going to last forever – Rob left the house with plenty of time to scour the charity shops on his local high street for heavy black pants and a couple of sweatshirts before taking the Metro transit system to Jesmond.

After the third and final shop he came to the conclusion that no-one wore black any more, so he headed to the station and into Newcastle and from there he would head towards the rehearsals.

Flynn Forbins, as he was known by his pen-name, was holding the telephone slightly tighter than he should have been. He was annoyed. His annoyance was exacerbated by the third tinny rendition of some banal pop ditty while he waited to be connected.

All he needed was one Arabic correction Mohgreb, phrase to compete Scene Four of Act One.

'Damn!' he exclaimed and slammed down the receiver, 'Bloody technology! What's wrong with people? Can't they just pick up a 'phone?'

He redialled the number.

After three rings it was answered with a sing-song voice: 'University, Sharon speaking, how may I help you?'

'Hello. Yes. Flynn Forbins. I am trying to get hold of Professor Vauxhall. He's doing some translation work for me and …'

'Connecting you …' interrupted the telephonist and the pop ditty started again.

'DAMN!'

'I fucking hate Christmas!' was Rob's greeting to Noodles as he and assorted carrier bags bundled through the double, half glazed doors of the rehearsal rooms of the church hall. He was fifteen minutes late. 'People with fat kids and fat shopping stuffing their fat mouths and dawdling!'

Noodles chuckled. 'Been doing some retail therapy have we?'

Rob dumped the carrier bags on a convenient old pew. 'Blacks and socks.'

Noodles shook his head and tutted. 'Should have said, Mate. I'd have got wardrobe to sort you some out. They've got stacks of extras for the U.V. scene.'

'Now you tell me! Sixty quid for a pair of Levis! Jeez, I was getting them in the States for forty dollars. Sorry I'm late; shoppers and bloody traffic.' He had run out of time during his foray into the thronging shops of the metropolis and had eventually flagged down a cab.

''S'okay. We're still waiting for a couple of the cast and the writer: "stuck in traffic",' Noodles offered by way of explanation. 'Time for a cuppa?' and led the way towards a battered door at the end of the hall.

A squat barrel of a man with heavy-set jowls and much receded, crew-cut hair was pouring water into a cup in the sparse kitchen of the church hall. He pushed his wire-rimmed glasses up his nose and turned to greet Rob and Noodles.

'Bit feckin' cold in here, Noodles. Can we see the verger or somebody and get the heating cranked?' he complained, 'And who's this?' His accent was mid-country, but without a burr, and venturing towards Queens English.

'Rob. Rob this is Alain; Alain, Rob. Alain's the director.'

The man nodded to Rob as he energetically dunked a tea-bag into the cup.

'Are they here yet?' asked Alain, 'I wouldn't mind getting on with this read-through. I want to finish at five.'

'Sounds like someone now,' Noodles replied, cocking his head towards the kitchen door and the sound of a sudden flurry of activity in the hall.

'Good, good. Onward and upward.' The tea bag was

unceremoniously thrown in the direction of an open-topped metal bin, where it hit the rim and splattered to the linoleum floor. The director took a slurp of the tea and pushed his way out into the rehearsal space.

'Afternoon, Darlings! Hope you've all brought your words as I ...' and then the self-closer snapped the door shut.

Rob grinned as Noodles looked slightly apologetic.

'Typical director,' Noodles observed.

'Yeah' Rob agreed, 'the turns and twirlies are "darlings" and we're just the boys in black.'

While Noodles was following up props leads and ordering them from suppliers, Rob had been following the script carefully and making margin notes.

> ABANAZER
> With one phrase I shall move this stone to reveal the cave behind it!

> ALADDIN
> Not that old hackneyed thing about 'Open Sesame'?

> ABANAZER
> (affronted) How do you know of this?

> ALADDIN
> Wishey worked in the Burger King bun section for a while.

> ABANAZER FACES THE ROCK AND SHOOTS HIS HANDS TOWARDS IT.

ABANAZER
Open Sesame!

ALADDIN
Sooo last century…

ABANAZER
If you know better, then you tell me, Boy!

ALADDIN LEANS TOWARDS ABANAZER AND WHISPERS
IN HIS EAR.

ABANAZER
You're sure?

ALADDIN NODS.
ABANAZER FACES THE ROCK AND SHOOTS HIS HANDS
TOWARDS IT.

ABANAZER
"123"

'Why have we still got this "one, two, three" thing?' demanded Alain.

'Ah, yes, sorry about that, but the translator still hasn't got back to me,' explained Flynn Forbins. 'I tried before I came out, but the Professor was… er… held up.'

'Right. But we'll have it in time?'

'Of course, Alain. Of course'

'Okay. Let's move on.'

Rob arrived back home at about six-thirty and after a swift conflab with Noodles, over a very mediocre pint in the Bodger; he made a cup of tea, sat down to go through the first day of the read-through and scan his notes. They had, eventually, reached the end of Act One – Aladdin had entered the cave:

ACT I - SCENE 5: THE CAVE

ALADDIN DESCENDS THE STAIRS INTO THE DARK
CAVE.
THE RING IS HIS ONLY ILLUMINATION (IRIS DOWN
F/SPOT).

ALADDIN
It's a bit spooky down here.

SKELETON TURNS HEAD TO LOOK AT HIM. AS HE
ADVANCES THOUGH CAVE MORE SKELETONS TURN TO
LOOK.

ALADDIN (to audience)
Ever get the feeling you're not alone?
Did you see anything?

SKELETONS ADVANCE ON ALADDIN

ALADDIN
Where?

AUDIENCE REACTION - PLAY ON REACTION UNTIL
EVENTUALLY BUMP INTO SKELETON.

                    ALADDIN
        Whoar! You're a … bones … thingy … Skeleton!

        SKELETONS SURROUND ALADDIN, PULL AT HIM AND
        THEN START DANCING *(poss Techno?)* ALADDIN HIDES.

        AT END OF DANCE SKELETONS ADVANCE ON ALADDIN.
            ALADDIN (FRIGHTENED) ASKS AUDIENCE:

                ALADDIN (TO AUDIENCE)
        Do you think if I rubbed the ring it would
        make it brighter and they would go away?

                ALADDIN RUBS RING.
        GENIE APPEARS AND SKELETONS SHY BACK AND EXIT.

He read on until the main Genie appeared and the curtain came down for the end of Act One.

Just as he returned the script to its folder the phone rang.

'Hello?'

All he could hear was a gasp, followed by heavy and laboured breathing.

'Hello?' he repeated.

A very faint voice said, 'Robert …'

'Lil?'

'… accident…'

Rob was on his feet in seconds, through the front door and up the path to his next door neighbour's. He hammered on the door for a full minute before a slight voice said, 'Keys… in the… jug…'

He knew exactly what Lil meant and ran back to his house and into the front room where a floral vase, stuffed with useless pens, cocktail stick umbrellas and various detritus was sitting on what was grandly called the china cabinet.

He upended the vase, tipping the contents onto the floor, and found what he was looking for – Lil's front door key.

Snatching at a key with a faded, brown cardboard label with '33' scrawled on it, he ran back to Lil's and let himself in.

The old lady was a crumpled heap at the bottom of the stairs; a dark red stain had spread from her lower back and soaked into the carpet.

'Jeez, Auntie Lil! What the hell?'

'Sorry Robert,' she apologised, 'I tried our Barry... but his phone...' then she gasped and passed out, her mobile phone clattering to the floor.

Rob pulled out his mobile and dialled three nines.

Rob sat in the A&E department for three and a bit hours until a very pretty nurse told him that they were "transferring his mother to the intensive care ward".

'But she's not my...' was all he had managed to say before being shepherded towards a lift.

'Level three,' instructed the nurse, 'Ward 32'.

He followed the signs to the ward and presented himself to the duty desk; it was suggested that he should take a seat in the waiting room.

Two hours later, and a good forty winks, he was gently shaken awake.

'Mister Crowther?' asked a uniform, 'You can see your mother now'.

Lil was propped up in the hospital bed on numerous pillows. She had oxygen pipes leading to her nose and various wires attached to her body that led to bleeping machines at the side of the bed.

Her eyes flicked open when Rob entered the room. 'Hello Robert' she greeted him, feebly.

Rob couldn't bring himself to speak. Someone he had known for almost his whole life was lying prostrate, grey and reduced to helplessness.

'It's alright Robert... Thank you...' she said, noticing the look upon his face.

'Lil...'

She waved a hand in his direction. 'Tsk...' she answered, dismissively, to the unasked question.

'You're feeling... 'y'know...?'

'Like shite,' she confirmed, and grinned.

'What happened?'

The old lady took a deep breath. 'I went for a wee, came out of the bathroom and took a dizzy. Next thing I know I'm at the bottom of the stairs.'

'D'you want me to phone your Barry?'

'I got one of the nurses to do that. He's offshore on a rig. North Sea. The company are sorting something...'

Rob knew that Lil's only child was a chef and that he had worked away from home for most of his adult life. 'So he's on his way?'

The old lady nodded twice: 'Couple of days. Aberdeen. Train...'

Rob nodded again, stuck for the words.

'Can I do anything? Nightie? Washbag?'

'That bottle of brandy would be good,' she replied, before creasing with pain as she was racked with a hacking cough.

'Lil?'

After a short pause to catch her breath she asked: 'Do you believe in ghosts Robert?'

'As in..?'

Ghosts. Do you believe in them?'

'I can't really... y'know...'

The old lady smiled. 'You do don't you?'

Rob's previous experience with the supernatural had been his seeing a blue light on a fly floor rail and a fly-bar being dropped onto a bad guy's head during the crews attempt to stop the REAG organisation from taking over the theatre and turning it into a bingo hall. 'Okay. What if I do?'

She smiled again: 'Your theatre has a lot of ghosts doesn't it?'

Rob shrugged.

'The grey lady?'

'Who?'

Lil closed her eyes for a moment before staring at Rob with her bright blue eyes: 'You know what I'm talking about…' she paused for a slight deep cough, 'The grey lady that's in the Upper Circle?'

Rob shrugged again and held out his hands in submission.

'My sister,' stated Lil.

'Your *sister*?'

She nodded.

'Dora was twelve years older than me so rather than being her little sister I was more like her daughter. Mother was too busy with the four boys. One night she said that she was going to the pictures, and that was the last we ever saw of her. 1953. The police didn't know who she was for a couple of days.' The old lady coughed again and then spat phlegm into a small polystyrene cup.

'Is this why you want to go to the theatre?' Rob knew the story of the woman found dead in a seat after a showing of "Gone With The Wind" when the theatre had been a cinema. Her throat had been cut from ear to ear.

Lil just nodded.

Rob took a deep breath.

'Don't you worry, Robert. I'll be fine. You promised to take me to the theatre at Christmas…' she took a gulp of air, '… I think it's time.' With that she closed her eyes and was immediately asleep.

The read-through and the rehearsals continued throughout the week and Rob was running around for some of the time, with Noodles and a Transit van, to collect props.

Every evening he visited the hospital to see if Lil's condition had improved. It had in one way, but not in others.

'Sorry to tell you Mister Crowther,' a nurse had explained, 'but your mother is very ill and there is not a lot we can do'. Rob had perpetuated the idea that he was Lil's son after the real thing had made a fleeting half hour visit, with a bunch of flowers and a bag of grapes, before returning to his job.

'I told Barry that I was okay,' explained Lil, 'and I was being looked after. No point his hanging around.'

Rob squeezed her hand.

'Anyway, the will is all sorted out but I don't think we'll be having that Christmas lunch.'

'Don't talk like that, Lil. You'll be fine. Plenty of years left in you yet'.

She just gave him an old-fashioned look and then closed her eyes.

'Ready for Sunday?' asked Noodles, as they loaded a large wicker laundry skip into the back of the Transit van.

'Guess so,' replied Rob, 'too bloody late now anyway, isn't it?'

'You'll be fine,' grinned Noodles, 'last of the geriatric crew.'

'Eh?'

Noodles laughed. 'I was sitting the other night going over the floor plans and the LX when I had a thought. Between us all we have nearly two hundred years of theatre experience. We really *should* be alright.'

'Two hundred?'

'If I include Tom, it's nearly *three* hundred,' he wickedly replied.

Rob cracked a grin. 'Don't you let him hear that! You'll get the usual "many a good tune, etcetera" line.'

DECEMBER

Rob waited, as instructed, in the recessed doorway, at the front of the theatre, under the canopy. "Noon, Sunday" Noodles had said. It was now a quarter past. Unless the foreign watch was doing the usual gain – possibly because of the freezing wind and the almost horizontal rain.

His mobile phone rang.

'Yeah?'

'Rob. We're in the Bodger. Bit of a delay. Where are you? Not like you to be off line or late?' It was Dickie.

'Freezing my arse off outside the theatre. Why did no-one ring?'

'What's this? Pigeon post?' chuckled the stage hand.

Rob beat a path to the pub, flipping his phone shut as he entered the much needed warmth of the public bar.

Val, the landlady, already had his Guinness half poured as he nudged his way through a small crowd interested in acquiring the rather large Sunday lunches that were on offer.

He took his foaming pint to the back table where the rest of the crew were assembled and, dragging up a chair, he sat himself down.

'Bit of a delay,' explained Dickie, 'Noodles has had to go and get keys from the manager. It sounds like she was pissed last night and wanted a lie-in, so he's jumped a cab. Shouldn't be long.'

'Anyone been to see if the wagon is on the dock?' asked Rob, checking that the set for the show had arrived outside the loading bay, before taking a long pull at his pint.

Before anyone could answer a, tall, stocky man drew up to the table and asked, through the upturned visor of his motorcycle helmet, 'Crew, I presume?'

He was dressed in a full leather body suit that made him stoop slightly, due to the fact that sitting on a motorbike took up less room than standing in a pub, and was equipped with biker boots and gloves to complete the ensemble.

'Hi. Yeah?' replied Foz.

The man removed his helmet to reveal a weatherworn, forty-something, face topped with a shaven head. He grinned.

'Harley' he stated by way of introduction, 'Noodles not here yet?' He then peeled off the heavy gloves and flipped them into the helmet.

He was met by a sea of blank faces.

'I guess Noodles didn't mention that I was joining this merry throng for the forty-nine Aladdins, the get-in the get-out and props?'

Fifteen minutes later, and after introductions and further beer, it transpired that Noodles had been phoned by Harley, who had just finished a short tour, and was looking for work. He had slotted him into the production and it seemed that Rob was to be more involved with helping to run the show than be a wingman.

'Do you smell that?' asked Rob, setting a foot onto the stage from the off-stage doorway.

'What? Smell what?' replied Foz.

'Nothing else smells like that.'

'What?'

Rob grinned. 'Theatre.'

'Aye,' agreed Tam, 'the smell o' th' crowd and th' roar o' the greasepaint'.

As the bevy of stagehands entered the loading dock area, Rob stopped short in his tracks and Dickie walked into his back.

'Jee-zuz! What a shit tip!' exclaimed Rob as he took in the rubbish that was piled against the walls, half covering the floor area. There were piles of discarded mineral water bottles, soft drink cans and empty snack packets along with the usual cast-offs of theatre. 'Does

REAG not look after this theatre?'

'Want a brush?' Dickie enquired wickedly, knowing that Rob had been the first on the clean-up after a show.

'It's not considered a theatre any longer, mate!' came Noodles' raised voice over the rattling of the dock's shutter door being raised. 'It's an MPEV.'

'A what?'

'MPEV. Multi Performance and Events Venue.'

'Bollocks. A theatre is what it says outside. Hell, I've seen tidier teenagers' bedrooms'.

A sudden fug of diesel fumes hit the air as the forty foot truck, its rear doors open and held back against its sides, reversed up to the dock to display the set contained within it. Wood, canvas, steel – and a good two hours' work.

As soon as the driver had stopped the vehicle, inches away from the platform, Noodles jumped onto a pile of yellow, polythene sacks. They would be stuffed with the hanging cloths. Further into the gloom, stacked against the walls, were the wooden pieces that would make up into flattage and between them were the smaller pieces and props.

'Right guys,' stated Noodles, taking charge, 'get the cloth-bags out and down to the fore-stage, the flattage against the walls and then everything else in the holding area'.

Rob braced his muscles, flexed his toes within his steel toe-capped boots and grabbed a bag.

'Well that wasn't three bad for a bunch of old bastards,' stated Dickie between licking the gum on a cigarette paper and rolling it around the tobacco.

'An' nae splinters,' observed Tam, looking closely at his hands.

'How about a cuppa before we hang the cloths?' asked Rob of Noodles.

'My thoughts exactly,' he replied, 'Dickie'll have to smoke outside, as will the rest of us. The whole theatre's non-smoking.'

'Y'know what?' asked Harley to no-one in particular, 'I reckon it's just a con.'

'What is?' asked Dickie, placing his roll-up behind his right ear.

'This no smoking ban thing. The guy that came up with "passive smoking is harmful" has come out and admitted that second-hand smoke has no effect on people. However, folk had jumped on the bandwagon and decided to ban it in public places. You know why?' without waiting for a reply he continued, 'Insurance.'

'Insurance?' Tam queried.

'Yup! Insurance. If you've got a venue or pub or office that's no smoking your insurance premiums will be lower.'

No one replied to this possible pearl of wisdom as Noodles led the band of stage techies off-stage.

Rob paused for a moment with the thought that this was not the way to the crew room, but decided to follow his co-workers down the ramp from the off-stage door and along a short corridor to where a door stood wedged open, with a paint splattered sink, some kitchen units and a shelf of coffee mugs in view within.

He went in and found that it was a corridor-type room with uncomfortable looking chairs against the walls and an alcove at the end containing some lockers. A single low wattage bulb lit the scene as Noodles flicked the switch on the kettle that stood on a small table behind the door.

'This used to be the stage store,' muttered Rob.

'Aye,' replied Tam overhearing, 'REAG upped oor sticks when they bought th' building next door. It's some beggar's kitchen noo'. He then slapped the wall halfway down the room and shouted, 'Gi' us back th' crew room!' and then sat down.

'So, no bunk-beds, no sofas and we live in this corridor for five weeks' Rob observed, sliding into one of the blue Hessian covered chairs, his knees almost touching Harley's, who sat opposite.

'Health and safety,' replied Noodles, 'they came up with the idea that sofas and bunks were a fire hazard'.

'Yeah! Right! Even though we Flambarred them.' Dickie stated, reminding everyone of the fireproofing spray that the furniture had been doused in every year.

'Doubt you'd be able to fit a sofa in here.' Rob stated, as he took the steaming mug of tea from Noodles.

Noodles spread the A1 sheet on the forestage and looked down at its contents: the hanging plot for the show.

'Simmy?' he shouted towards the fly floor, thirty-odd feet above stage left.

'Yeah?' came back the girl's reply.

'Lets have bar forty and we'll hang the Cyc. Then I want...' he consulted the plan, '... thirty-four and thirty'.

'kay!' came back the answer as she released the brake on the single purchase pulley system and the requested flying bar lowered into sight from the grid some seventy feet above. It swayed gently as it rested four feet above the stage.

As the off-white cyclorama was lifted to the bar, all hands were quickly at work, tying it off to the bar from the central red tie-tab. From the fly floor the clanging of 25 kilo weights being loaded into the counterweight cradle was the only noise.

As soon as the last tie-off was fastened Simmy was given the go-ahead to take the bar out to the grid.

'What's on thirty-four?' asked Harley as the required bar started to descend.

'Peking Street' replied Noodles.

They turned over several of the cloth bags to show their labels until they came across the bag they needed.

Just as the last cloth, the show cloth labelled *Aladdin*, was being flown out on the foremost downstage bar, the off-stage door opened and three men entered.

Rob recognised them from the rehearsals.

The first was over six feet tall and of stocky build with shoulder length blond hair and a thick moustache gracing his upper lip; Dan O'Leary, who was to play Wishey Washee. He was followed by the duo of Bigg 'n' Liddle, real names Paul and Michael, as Rob had learned at the rehearsal rooms. It turns out that they had actually put up the money for the show and were therefore titled "The Producers" in the programme; a box of these had split open whilst he and Noodles had been loading them into the Transit van from the pick up at the printers, and Rob had read one with interest.

'All up. Excellent!' grinned Liddle.

'Any problems, Noodles?' asked Bigg.

Dan O'Leary just looked up and followed out the ascent of the cloth.

'There... er ... may be,' was the reply.

'Oh?' snatched the stocky comic.

'I don't know what was ordered, Dan, but I'm sure that parts of it are not Aladdin.'

'Show me.'

'Bar twenty!' shouted Noodles towards the fly floor.

As the cloth slowly descended the trio of producers joined Noodles on the forestage.

The bottom hem of the cloth had hardly touched the stage when O'Leary exclaimed: 'Eh? What the hell is that?'

'Palace garden backing,' replied Noodles.

'Where! On planet fucking Zog?'

The cloth, twenty-five feet high and stretching forty feet to the wings of the stage, was garishly painted with an orange and pink sky, lime green foliage on purple trunked trees and someone's idea of grass lands – in pale blue.

'Not what I ordered,' stated Bigg, starting to reach for his mobile phone.

'Any other "Star Trek" surprises?' asked Liddle.

'Take that and give me twenty-two,' instructed Noodles to the fly-floor.

The offending cloth was raised to be replaced by another further up the stage.

The four men watched the cloth descend whilst Rob and the others hovered in the wings.

'Where, in Aladdin, is there a fucking Cinderella kitchen?' demanded O'Leary, reaching for his mobile phone and pointing it at the offending cloth to take a photograph.

'It's supposed to be the Twanky cloth for the laundry,' explained Noodles.

'Can't get through to the suppliers,' interjected Bigg, folding his mobile.

'Any *more* surprises?' Liddle asked.

'Nothing that can't be fixed.'

'Like?'

'Flys! Show gauze, please. All the way.'

The cloth with the legend slowly made its way to the stage and past the in-dead.

'Hold it there!' Noodles instructed, as the cloth reached over two thirds of the way onto the stage. He pointed up towards the legend and above it a gaping rip. 'We can fix it with needle and thread,' he assured them.

'Get the drinks please, Rob' instructed O'Leary, having calmed down, cleaned up and adjourned to the Bodger. 'I'll have a large white wine.' He passed Rob two twenty pound notes as he sat down next to Noodles at the head of the large table.

As he made his way to the corner of the bar Rob couldn't help grinning to himself. Producers were the same the world over, and he'd met a few; the slightest thing seemed to throw them. They were just not of the mindset that "shit happens". Come tomorrow evening, and after a few phone calls, the correct cloths would be express-delivered by a courier and by the time they had the rest of the set built and in place the two cloths would have been received at stage door and then flown. No doubt *he* would get the job of stitching the gauze.

Once everyone had a drink in front of him, O'Leary placed both hands on the table and made a move to stand. He obviously had second thoughts and addressed the assembly sitting down. 'Thank you for today, boys and girls; I'm just sorry that it didn't go as planned. Paul will get onto the suppliers first thing and I'll e-mail them when I get back home. Let's just hope that tomorrow will belong to us. Cheers!' He raised his glass in salute.

Little did he know that things were going to get worse.

Professor James Aloysius Vauxhall, head of the Eastern Languages department, took a moment to push his glasses up to his hairline, rub his eyes and lean back onto his suit jacket which was slung over the back of his swivel chair. He glanced at the clock on his study mantelpiece and noticed that it was only nine-oh-five. He had been studying the ancient script before him since six that morning.

His telephone rang and he reached to answer it.

'Vauxhall,' he stated.

'Ah! Professor. Finally. Sorry to ring so early but it's about the passage you promised me?' said the caller. 'Aladdin?'

'Oh yes, its ... Dobbins isn't it?'

'Forbins. Flynn Forbins. I was wondering if you had the passage ready for me?'

Vauxhall pinched his nose and sighed inwardly. He had not given the request for the translation a thought since being asked by one of his students on the writers' behalf.

'What was the passage again?'

'"I bring to life the stone to do my bidding."'

'Hmm… You do realise that it would not be a direct translation due to the nuances of the language?'

'Of course, of course. However, it's imperative that I have it today as we start the rehearsals proper tomorrow.'

The academic again pinched his nose and rattled off an Arabic sounding phrase.

'Sorry could you say that again – only slower because I'm writing it down.'

The Professor repeated what he had said.

As the line went dead he had a thought about what he had said to the writer.

'Damn!' he exclaimed, again rubbing his eyes. 'Oh, never mind, he'll never know'.

At the same time as the writer was typing his newly translated line into the pantomime script the actual physicality of the production was starting to take shape.

'Okay…' instructed Noodles, '…let's get the mountain pass, cave thingy, frontage up. Then we'll break for a brew.'

'Still hav'nae found the flyin' wires.' shouted Tam from the dock area where he had been searching through large plastic tubs and laying out the hardware for the set since before nine o'clock that morning.

'Bollocks! What have you got?'

The Scotsman held up a bundle of steel wires all neatly, and separately, taped together: 'Four. You said six.'

'Lets get it laid out, Mate, and then we can jerry-rig it if we haven't got the stuff.' suggested Rob.

Noodles nodded and the crew set about lifting large pieces of wooden scenery from the walls in the wings out to their appropriate place on the stage, and laying them flat and face down. They were all marked up, on the rear, with theatre parlance that all could understand; PS for prompt side; OP for opposite prompt; CS for centre stage and each piece of the jigsaw that went between these was marked with arrows pointing to its partner.

It was not long before all the pieces were laid out side-to-side and the flattage fastened together with hinges and pins; strengthening battens were laid horizontally across the whole piece.

Suddenly every light – above and to the sides of stage, some behind the proscenium arch – lit up.

'Whoa!' several voices exclaimed as hands shaded eyes.

'I'm melting …' exclaimed a lone female voice from above, in her best "Wicked Witch of the West" voice.

Noodles turned to the auditorium. 'Pendry! For fucks sake! Give us a warning if you're going to do that!'

'Sorry,' came the sing-song voice of the Welsh, REAG electrician. 'Just thought you might like a bit more light.'

The Welshman had been sitting in the crew room when they had all turned up that morning. He was of slight build but sported an enormous growth on his upper lip that looked as if a scrubbing brush had attached itself to him. Rob had noticed immediately that he had a habit of grooming the moustache as he spoke.

'Just drop it down will you please,' instructed Noodles.

The lights dimmed to about fifty percent of their former brightness and some were extinguished altogether.

'Better,' stated Dickie.

'Looks like we can hang this on the four wires and use ropes for the intermediates,' observed Rob, nudging the large piece with his boot.

'You're right,' agreed Noodles, 'outers and inners wired.' He glanced up at the fly floor and then shouted, 'Simmy! Dive up the grid and drop us a couple of lines right in, will you?'

'Okay boss' was the girl's reply.

'You'll have to wear hard hats' was Pendry's instruction from the darkened auditorium.

As one, all heads turned towards the voice and stared.

It was Dickie who broke the silence. 'Fuck. Off!'

'I'm just saying. It's company policy. Anyone on the grid then stage boys should wear hard hats. Health and Safety.' He capitalised the words.

'Have you ever seen what'll happen if you drop a shackle from the grid?' asked Rob into the darkness.

'Erm…'

'Thought not. It'll go straight through the hat and half way into your head.' Turning away he muttered, 'Burk.'

Within half an hour the large piece had been rope-tied and wired and shackled to the flying bar and then everyone had gathered around it to help support the flying-out process.

Once it was in the air Noodles shouted, 'TEA!'

'Not that much left to do, I guess?' asked Rob, dragging on a roll-up outside the stage door.

Noodles exhaled smoke into the increasingly cold afternoon. It was hardly possible to distinguish between smoke and breath. 'Not much. Build the finale walk-down and then tidy up.' He glanced at his watch. 'Should be finished by seven.'

The replacement cloths had arrived just before they were due to break and had been hung immediately. Noodles had rung O'Leary to let him know, and he was due for a visit any time soon with the writer, who wanted a look-see before the start of the walkthrough with the cast that was scheduled for the following morning.

'Would all cast and crew please assemble on stage in five minutes please,' rang out from the Tannoy. It was Sam's voice.

'No' bad at all,' stated Tam, glancing at his watch. 'Nine o'clock call an' th' cast get t' start an hour later.'

'Turns and twirlies, Mate, turns and twirlies.' Dickie did not look up from his book.

'There's got to be better collective nouns for this lot, y'know,' observed Harley.

'Like?' came the chorus.

'Well, what do you call a bunch of dancers? Twirlies. How about a fumble of twirlies? Turn out the lights and they're lost.'

'Aye. No' bad. Ah'd a thought of a wallet of Producers?'

Pendry mumbled something.

'What was that?' asked Rob.

'A whinge of techies,' the Welshman grinned.

'Aye, an' a short o' electricians,' Tam threw back at him.

'A block of directors?' Rob suggested.

'C'mon boys, stage' ordered Noodles.

'Ah! A command of tech managers.' observed Dickie, closing his volume onto a bus ticket book-mark and smiling.

A small table, together with a few bottles of water and three seats, had been place on the forestage and sitting centre was Alain, the director, and to his left Flynn Forbins. Dan O'Leary was sitting on one end of the table in conversation with the other two comedians.

Cast, dancers and crew finally assembled centre stage and the chatter died down when Alain spoke.

'Morning, morning, morning,' he greeted, 'out of the frying pan and into the firing line, eh?'

A slight titter was heard from the dancers.

Breaking into a grin, and standing, he continued, 'I want to do a walkthrough this morning so that we can block in some of the moves, then run some of the scene changes after lunch. Flynn has amended scripts for you; you should have found them in your dressing rooms.' He looked around for reassurance and confirmation and several heads bobbed.

'Good. The opening number is the song and dance but I don't intend to go there yet as the band's not installed until later. I'd like to start with Act One, Scene Three; Twankey's entrance. Anyone not involved please return to the dressing rooms and Sam will call you as needed. Thanks.' The grin faded.

'Bollocks!' muttered Noodles, 'they'll want the laundry skip and I've not finished modding it yet.'

'Where is it?' Rob asked.

'Dock. C'mon, we'll get it on stage.'

As the two men pushed the large wicker basket from the loading dock area and into the wings Alain raised his voice. 'Noodles, skip please.'

'Coming…'

The prop was placed centre stage with the lid open.

'Okay, Dan. Let's start with you having fallen in. Jimmy can be in the wing.' He nodded towards the actor that was to be "dragged up" as the dame.

TWANKY ENTERS WITH BULGING SHOPPING BAGS.

TWANKEY:
Yoo-hoo! Wishey! I'm home!

WISHEY STANDS UP - HE HAS A SET OF BLOOMERS
ON HIS HEAD.
WISHEY:
(muffled voice) Hello mum. Been shopping?

TWANKEY STARES AT WISHEY FOR A MOMENT THEN
SEARCHES HER SHOPPING.

TWANKEY:
I knew I'd forgotten something.

WISHEY QUICKLY REMOVES THE BLOOMERS FROM HIS
HEAD AND DROPS THEM IN THE SKIP.

WISHEY:
Looks like you bought everything in town.

TWANKEY:
I got some amazing bargains. Mataland had
fifty percent off everything. Look.

SHE PULLS THE LEFT HALF OF A DRESS (ON A
HANGER) FROM A CARRIER BAG.

WISHEE:
I suppose you're spent up? I was hoping for
my pocket money cos there's a new game for the
Why-Aye I wanted to get.

TWANKEY:
Weeee

WISHEY:
Upstairs and second door on the left.

TWANKEY:
No, no. It's pronounced 'We'.

WISHEY PONDERS FOR A BEAT OR TWO AND PULLS
FROM THE SKIP AN EMPTY SOAP POWDER BOX.

WHISHEY:
I bet you forgot to buy more soup?

ALADDIN (OFFSTAGE):
Quick … quick!

ALADDIN RUNS ON STAGE.

ALADDIN:
Quick, hide me! The coppers are chasing me!

WISHEY INDICATES THE SKIP AND ALADDIN JUMPS
IN PULLING THE LID CLOSED. WISHEY SITS ON THE
SKIP.

ENTER POLICEMEN WITH TRUNCHEONS DRAWN.

POLICEMAN PING:
You sure he ran in here, Officer Pong?

POLICEMAN PONG:
I am, Officer Ping.

PING:
Widow Twankey, we shall have to search your
location.

TWANKEY SMILES AND HOLDS UP HER ARMS AS IF
WANTING TO BE FRISKED.

TWANKEY:
Ooh! Best offer I've had all day.

PONG:
No, no, the *premises*. Your Aladdin dared to
look at the Princess Su Duk-oh and we have to
arrest him. He'll get ASBO'd for this.

(PONG STARTS TO SEARCH)

WISHEY:
I though looking at the Princess meant you
got your head chopped off?

PING:
That's what he said. ASBO'd. A Slight Bend
Over and then … (MAKES CHOPPING MOTION WITH HIS
TRUNCHEON).

PONG APPROACHES LAUNDRY SKIP AND TRIES TO
LIFT LID. WISHEY STAYS SEATED.

PONG:
Only place left to look.

'Okay! Let's hold it there.' The director came around the table
and stood in front of the skip. 'When you lift Wishey off …' he
pondered for a moment, 'Wishey, can you sit cross-legged on top of
the skip? Then the guys can lift you off still cross legged.'
Heads nodded.
'Okay, let's run that again.'
'This,' observed Dickie, who was leaning up against the stage left

wall, near the prompt desk, 'is going to be a long morning.'

'That was a long three hours,' observed Harley, 'Christ knows if we'll get up to Scene Four.'

'I had a word with Alain,' assured Noodles, 'and he wants to go straight into the mountain pass bit for the cave after lunch. That should give us a bit of leeway. Twirlie stuff after that.' He then shovelled a large forkful of steak and ale pie into his mouth.

'At least the rock works now,' added Rob. He had spent several hours with Noodles attempting to get the painted, three dimensional piece of 20mm plywood to run smoothly on its pelmet and castors in order to effect the illusion of a boulder rolling back from the cave entrance so that Aladdin could go and retrieve the lamp.

'It's sticking on the LX.' shouted Sam from the fly floor, 'can I have someone up here and I'll stick a brail on it?'

The mountain pass scenery had caught three times on the lighting as the girl had tried to bring it into stage – the problem was the door catching on trailing cables.

'Rob. Dive up, please' Noodles instructed. 'Sorry, Alain, just be a couple of minutes,' he explained.

A rope was lowered to the stage level as Rob ran up the five flights of stairs to the fly floor. At the third level he had to stop. 'Friggin' hell.' he gasped, 'I used to get up here without thinking.' As well as feeling out of breath his steel toe-capped boots felt like lead weights. He waded slowly and painfully up the remaining two flights to the fly floor door and yanked at the handle. The door didn't move.

'What..?' He noticed a punch-button lock next to the handle and not having a clue what the code was he just hammered on the door.

A moment or two passed before Simmy answered it.

'Which fuck-wit put that on?' was Rob's greeting.

'Oh it's the REAG lot. They think somebody's going to pinch the fly floor.'

'Health. And. Safety?' stressed Rob.

The girl just grinned in agreement and led the way onto the flying area. Rob crossed the bridge that ran over the proscenium arch and onto the hemp fly floor on the stage left side. Using a series of nods, finger signals and another rope the scenery was pulled inches up stage and the ropes cleated off.

Sam then slowly attempted to send the flattage onto stage. It landed softly and immediately actors were petting it as if it were a toy dog.

Rob crossed over the bridge and made his way to the stage.

ACT I - SCENE 4: A MOUNTAIN RAVINE

ENTER ABANAZER FOLLOWED BY ALADDIN. THEY ARE
FIGHTING AGAINST A STRONG WIND.

ALADDIN:
(Whinging) Are we there yet?

ABANAZER:
(Frustrated) Aagh! Almost.

ALADDIN:
You never said it would be this flipping cold!

ABANAZER:
Will you stop complaining!

PAUSE. CROSS STAGE TO CS.

ALADDIN:
(*Whinging*) Are we there yet?

THEY APPROACH A LARGE STONE WHICH COVERS A
CAVE.

ABANAZER:
This is the place.

ALADDIN:
What? A big rock?

ABANAZER:
That which we seek is behind the rock.

ALADDIN: (LOOKS AT A LARGE COMPASS WHICH HE
IS CARRYING AROUND HIS NECK ON A ROPE)
It sits north.

ABANAZER:
It does?
ALADDIN:
We have to move this to see what is behind
it?

ABANAZER:
… or make it fall away.

ALADDIN:
I don't think the economy could stand that a
second time.

ABANAZER:
What?

ALADDIN:
A second collapse of the Northern Rock.

ABANAZER:
(frustrated) Boy! I shall use magic to move the rock!

ALADDIN:
That's what Richard Branston said.

ABANAZER:
With one phrase I shall move this stone to reveal the cave behind it!

ALADDIN:
Not that old hackneyed thing about Open Sesame?

ABANAZER:
(affronted) How do you know of this?

ALADDIN:
Wishey worked in a burger bar bun section for a while.

ABANAZER FACES THE ROCK AND SHOOTS HIS HANDS TOWARDS IT.

ABANAZER:
Open Sesame!

ALADDIN:
Sooo last century…

ABANAZER:
If you know better then you tell me boy!

ALADDIN LEANS INTO ABANAZER AND WHISPERS IN
HIS EAR.

ABANAZER:
You're sure?

ALADDIN NODS.
ABANAZER FACES THE ROCK AND SHOOTS HIS HANDS
TOWARDS IT.

The following words were hardly out of the actor's mouth when the writer jumped up. 'No. NO! That's not how it's pronounced!' Flynn Forbins was on his feet and advancing towards Abanazer. 'You need to use more inflection! It's an old form of Arabic. Think Middle East!'

Frank Gartiner, who was playing Abanazer with his usual gusto, merely stepped back. 'I just got the words this morning and…'

Yes, yes. Sorry. You say it like this: "Ana ahzer ela hayat altmtheil an etim bedengh" Okay?'

The actor nodded.

On the street below the façade of the theatre a small shower of dust floated towards the pavement.

'*Something just happened.*'

'*Mama?*'

'*Bertie. Something just happened. I felt it.*'

'*What do you mean, Mother?*'

'*I… I don't know. I felt something… move. Almost as if the fabric of the building… shuddered.*'

'*Shuddered?*'

'*Please do not repeat what I say Bertie. Something has happened to this theatre!*'

'Sorry, sorry. Can we stop there?' Alain stood, moved upstage to the scenery, and then turned to the writer. 'Flynn, I know you've spent some time doing the script but I really don't like this Arabic bit. It's not… traditional. Let's just go with the "Open Sesame".'

'But…' the writer started to object.

'Changes, changes, Flynn. There will probably be a few more as we go on. Additions. Subtractions.' The director placed a full faced grin on his visage, 'Theatre…' he said by way of explanation.

'But…'

'Right, let's continue.'

'That was a loooong day,' Rob observed before he took his first sip of Guinness at seven-fifteen that evening.

Several heads nodded but Noodles just grinned.

'Ma feet feel like…' Tam started

'Shite?' suggested Dickie.

'Aye.'

'Geriatrics.' smiled Noodles.

'Talking about me again, you bitches?' asked Tom joining the company.

All heads turned towards the stage door keeper cum spotlight operator.

'I don't know. just coz I get to a certain age…' he sat down at the table.

'Checked out your spot yet?' asked Noodles.

Tom nodded whilst taking a sip of his real ale: 'Went up there this afternoon and checked out things. Same as usual - apart from the bloody seagull or whatever it was.'

'Seagull?' Rob asked.

'Just as we did the cave scene – and that old poof Flynn put his oar in – there was a … a sort of flapping up in the Gods. Bloody seagull must have got in through the roof again. Mind you, it had eyes like a shit house rat.'

Tam, halfway through a mouthful of lager, spluttered and then caught his breath as fluid spurted from his nostrils: 'A wha'?'

'Shit house rat,' reiterated Tom. 'Old term. You wouldn't understand.'

'Seagull? What? Got in through the roof?' Foz asked.

'Age old problem,' explained Tom. 'Always been there, always will.' He took another sup of his ale.

'What do you mean about the eyes?' asked Rob.

The pensioner placed his glass very carefully onto a soggy beer mat: 'As I was watching the cave scene I heard a noise from the back of the Gods. Thought it was just the wind, or something. As they ran through the scene and into the cave bit this… thing… flapped behind me and as I turned to look it sloped off but it looked directly at me. Shit house rat eyes.'

Rob just nodded.

The next day the call was for nine in the morning and dutifully the whole crew turned up and hung the side masking black legs, finished making the walk-down structure for the finale of the pantomime, put a large props table at the crossover point – behind the cyc – built the quick change area in the upstage position and laid carpet runners down each wing of the stage. By lunchtime they were all assembled in the crew room and slipping on coats to go to the local sandwich, pizza or burger shops – lunch, such as it was, was to be only a half hour.

'Act One, Scene One. From the top, please. All cast on stage at one-thirty,' Sam's voice echoed through the Tannoy.

'An' ah bet we dinnae dae a jot until two,' was Tam's take on the announcement.

By one-forty several musicians had appeared in the pit at the front of the stage, with the usual drum-kit, guitars, organs and assorted percussion.

Pendry, who had worked through the lunch break, had added standing boom lights to the positions behind the black masking legs, pyrotechnic pots into the well on the forestage and the props table had been filled with "carry-ons" that had been marked out with their holding positions by Harley.

A sound company had also obviously been in and installed the PA system and onstage microphones, as was evident by the "floats" on the fore-stage.

The cast and dancers had arrived in dribs and drabs on the stage – some of them wearing half costume. Jimmy Wands was now sporting a huge over-the- shoulder pair of false breasts encompassed in heavy linen, and he nudged them every now and again, with his elbow.

'Have we sorted out that the genie traps are safe?' asked Alain to Noodles, who was standing at the table still positioned on the forestage.

'Rob, Foz and Tam are down there now,' he reassured, ' ...should be no problem.'

Frank Gartiner, a long time actor who loved playing villains, joined Rob and the rest of the trap crew under stage whilst the rest of the production assembled above.

'Frank.' nodded Rob by way of greeting.

The actor studied the contraption for sending him through the stage. The same machinery had been used since Victorian times, if not before, and was all part of the theatrical illusion of sudden appearance.

He would step up onto a counterweighted platform, just under two feet square; one of the crew would open a sliding trapdoor in the stage just before another two crewmen would haul on ropes to send him shooting stage-wards, all to be accompanied by suitable music and a flash-bang pyrotechnic from the forestage.

'How do you like it?' grinned Rob.

Frank knew exactly what he meant. 'Let's not do "atomic" for the first go.'

Pseudo-Chinese music drifted through the wall and was finalised with a crash from a large gong in the pit. The music then segued into the opening song and dance number.

Twirlies were giving it their all as tap shoes beat out a regular rhythm on the boards above the trap crew's heads and the company burst into song.

Moments later muffled police whistles blew and Rob knew it was almost time.

The cue-light box blinked its red "stand-by" on and off and Foz acknowledged the signal by pressing the small button and turning the lamp to a constant red.

'Up you go, Frank,' said Rob as he helped the tall actor onto the wooden platform; it wobbled slightly as he stepped up.

'I do hope you have the break on,' he warbled in slight panic.

'Locked on,' Foz assured him.

The comedians' patter above them could be just heard in the under-stage area as Tam slid the vertical bar holding the trap cover from the "safe" position to the "action" one.

Foz and Rob took position with a high grip on the ropes that would move the platform and actor to stage level as soon as the cue light flicked to green.

Footsteps ran off to stage right above them. Police whistles blew. Green!

With previously rehearsed precision Tam pulled back on the bar, dropping the piece of stage onto a slider; it drew back to reveal a twenty-two square inch hole above the trap: 'Clear!'

They heaved on the ropes and the actor on his platform shot stage-wards.

Tam pulled another lever. 'Locked' he reported.

The team moved to the stage right trap that mirrored that which the baddie had just gone through.

'She's going to miss the cue,' stated Foz.

'Aye,' Tam agreed.

The cue light blinked red, it was acknowledged and they waited. Green.

'Hold it! Hold it!' Alain's muffled voice could be heard from above and then a stamped foot, twice, on the trap cover.

Tam slid it open and Alain's face appeared through it: 'Problem?' asked the director.

'No Genie of the Ring,' Rob stated, looking up.

The face disappeared to a shout of, 'Sam! Where is she?'

At that moment one of the girl dancers came into view wearing golden pantaloons and curly-toed Eastern slippers. She burst through the under-stage door holding a spangled gold bra-top to her chest.

'Sorry, sorry. My fault. I couldn't get this bloody thing to stay fastened,' she said by way of explanation, holding out the back-straps to the costume.

'Aye, weel, it's no like y're a little girl, is i'?' Tam cheekily grinned.

'Alain!' shouted Rob through the still open hole.

The head re-appeared.

'Costume malfunction. Looks like you're going to get a bare-chested Genie.' Rob kept a perfectly straight face as he looked up, knowing that the girl was now standing next to him with the errant top dangling from her index finger.

Without a second glance the director's head vanished to the shout of: 'Wardrobe!'

'Y' brazen hussy!' Tam chortled.

'Oh, I know, I know,' giggled the girl, skipping off towards the door, holding the top to her ample breasts again.

The smell of freshly brewed coffee wafted from the crew room door as Rob, Tam and Foz approached it just after three o'clock.

'Harley,' stated Foz, sniffing the air. 'He said he was going to do "proper" coffee.'

The small table behind the door now held a gurgling percolator as well as the kettle.

'May as well feel at home,' Harley grinned.

'How's that?' Noodles asked.

'I'd be doing nothing and have the coffee on.'

'So y' missed th' second malfunction, eh?' Tam asked.

'Nope. Nice tits,' came the reply. 'Loved the nipples.' he grinned.

On the second attempt to get the Genie of the Ring through the trap door everything had gone to plan. Red; green; slider; trap.

It wasn't until half way through the girl's lines that the costume had decided to strain at its fastenings and accelerate towards the fore-stage.

ABANAZER:
I would have you tell me how I may acquire
the lamp that I so greatly desire?

GENIE OF THE RING:
You must seek a boy in a far off land...

She made this announcement with a suitable and extravagant arm gestures and, in a manner reminiscent of a Carry-On film, the unreliable costume top flew off, landing at Flynn Forbin's feet.

The scribe blushed fiercely and while Alain scrambled to retrieve the flimsy object the girl crossed her arms to cover Flynn's embarrassment, if not her own. The writer grabbed a pen and scribbled in his book.

'Coffee?' Harley held up the now prepared pot of Java.

There were several takers but Rob stuck to a cup of tea, never having been a great fan of coffee unless brandy or a similar liqueur was involved.

'Ready for the cave scene?' asked Noodles, accepting a mug of the steaming brew.

Simmy, knowing that she had to navigate the brail-line, nodded, as did the rest.

'Good. We might get finished by seven.'

Rob was standing at the prompt desk, down-stage left, looking over Sam's shoulder as she tried to cue-up everything for the scene transformation: from the external entrance to the cave on the mountain pass into the haunted interior of the cave. Dancers and Babes (the 'under elevens' that were seconded from the stage-school to play non-speaking and dance parts) had to be ready as had the Genie of the Lamp – understage – and Simmy on the fly floor.

'Y' okay, Sam?' Rob enquired.

The girl nodded whilst giving instructions over her "cans" – the headset intercom system.

'I'll go do the trap,' said Rob as he slipped away.

Walking up to the off-stage door he soundlessly swung it open, walked the few feet to a door on his left, descended two flights and pulled open the door marked "Understage".

The blue working lights were already on and Tam and Foz lounged next to the trap that was to be used for the Lamp Genie – the same one that the Ring Genie had shot up. With them was Paul Bigg who was doubling up his "Policeman" role with that of the genie.

The actor's make-up had changed from a toothbrush moustache, strongly painted eyebrows and kohl at the corner of his eyes – to accentuate the thinness – to an oriental goatee. He was wearing only a turban, a loincloth and gold boxing boots.

'Knicker elastic strong enough?' Rob grinned.

The actor placed his thumbs into the waistband of his costume: 'Oh yes, don't want the old warhorse popping out, do we?' he grinned back.

Foz idly rubbed the side of his nose: 'More like a pit pony someone told me.'

The actor stepped up to the trap: 'Aye. Well. It has been in some dark inhospitable places...' he smiled.

During the tea break someone, presumably Pendry, had placed a set of cans, on a long lead, next to the trap. Rob placed them over his head and adjusted them so that only one ear-muff was in position.

'Pit's on standby,' came Sam's voice. 'Stand-by LX; stand-by sound; stand by flys.'

There was obviously no problem as she then fell quiet and seconds later the vibrato from the orchestra pit started and muffled voices could be heard from above:

```
ABANAZER:
This is the place.
```

ALADDIN:
What? A big rock?

ABANAZER:
That which we seek is behind the rock.

ALADDIN: (TAKES COMPASS FROM AROUND NECK)
It sits north.

ABANAZER:
It does?

ALADDIN:
We have to move this to see what is behind
it?

ABANAZER:
… or make it fall away.

ALADDIN:
I don't think the economy could stand that a
second time.

ABANAZER:
What?

ALADDIN:
A second collapse of the Northern Rock.

ABANAZER:
(frustrated) Boy! I shall use magic to move
the rock!

ALADDIN:
That's what Richard Branson said.

ABANAZER:
With one phrase I shall move this stone to reveal the cave behind it!

ALADDIN:
Not that old hackneyed thing about Open Sesame?

ABANAZER:
(affronted) How do you know of this?

ALADDIN:
Wishey worked in a burger bar bun section for a while.

ABANAZER FACES THE ROCK AND SHOOTS HIS HANDS TOWARDS IT.

ABANAZER:
Open Sesame!

ALADDIN:
Sooo last century…

ABANAZER:
If you know better then you tell me boy!

ALADDIN LEANS INTO ABANAZER AND WHISPERS IN
HIS EAR.

ABANAZER:
Utter rubbish! I shall use what the sages of
old have always used!

ABANAZER: (MORE INTENSE)
Open Sesame!

THE ROCK SLOWLY MOVES TO THE SIDE TO REVEAL A
CAVE ENTRANCE.

ALADDIN CUPS HIS HANDS TO HIS MOUTH AND SHOUTS
INTO CAVE.

ALADDIN:
Yoo-hoo… Mister Bin Laden…?

ABANAZER:
Wrong!... This is the entrance to an object
that I seek. The lamp that I told you of.
Descend the stairs and we shall be rich when you
return.

ALADDIN STICK HIS HEAD THROUGH THE CAVE
ENTANCE AND THEN TURNS TO ABANAZER

ALADDIN:
Looks a bit spooky to me… and dark.

ABANAZER:
Just go down the stairs. It will get lighter in the cave. Once you are there look for a lamp – do not touch anything else. Nothing but the lamp!

ALADDIN MAKES TO CROSS THE CAVE THRESHOLD BUT PAUSES FOR A MOMENT.

ALADDIN:
Just the lamp?

ABANAZER:
Just the lamp.

ALADDIN ENTERS THE CAVE ENTRANCE.

ALADDIN:
Aladdin the cave.

ABANAZER:
Ha! Ha! Soon my plans will all come together! The stupid boy will get me the lamp and I shall rule all before me! Ha! Ha! Ha!

ALADDIN JUMPS OUT OF THE CAVE.

ALADDIN:
A lad out the cave.

ABANAZER:

Do not test me boy! Go and get the lamp!

ALADDIN:
It's really dark down there. There's spiders
and bats and ghoulies and ghosties and things
that might go bump. I need a light.

ABANAZER THROWS UP HIS HANDS IN FRUSTRATION.

ABANAZER:
Take this. (REMOVES RING FROM FINGER AND
PASSES IT TO ALADDIN) It will give a small
glow when you enter the darkness. It should be
enough.
Now get me the lamp!

ALADDIN ENTERS THE CAVE.

ALADDIN:
It's a bit dark down here…

ABANAZER: (into cave)
Hold the ring in front of you. It will help.
Does it glow?

ALADDIN:
It's glowing.

ABANAZER: (to audience)
At last! At last! (LAUGHS)

'Fly cue go!' instructed Sam over the headset just as the understage door opened and the Ring Genie entered. She was now wearing a gold halter-top, the bra having been decided as too risky in front of a bunch of ten year old lads'n'dads.

She stepped up to the trap and without a word climbed onto it just as the red "stand-by" started to flash.

Suddenly there was an ear-piercing scream from above and cries of, "Stop! Stop!"

Rob ran as fast as he could from the understage position to the side of stage to be greeted with half the cast standing looking up.

'What..?' he demanded. Noodles grabbed him and ran towards the doors in the direction of the fly-floor.

'C'mon… Simmy's just fallen over…'

'What! Fallen over the fly rail?' he panted as he followed the tech manager up the flights of stairs.

Noodles paused to punch in the key code for the door but in his haste he bungled it and had to have a second attempt. He and Rob raced to the fly floor rail and looked over.

Ten feet below them Simmy was dangling by a rope looped around her ankle. On stage someone, it looked like Foz from where they were, had dragged out the Tallescope – an extendable ladder on a carriage system – and was busily deploying it.

'Simmy?' shouted Noodles, 'Simmy, are you okay?'

The girl didn't move or answer him.

Rob checked the line that was holding the girl. It was the rope that had been changed from a brail-line on the flattage to a brail-line on the lighting so that the cave scenery could move without snarling on wires. The cleat that was holding the line was as solid as any other.

'Foz!' shouted Noodles, 'how you doing?'

The rattle of the ladder being extended greeted his question, before he replied 'Okay, but I don't think this is going to reach.'

Ever a quick thinker in times of danger or in one of the "shit happens" moments, Rob grabbed a spare rope from a nearby cleat, tied it off on one end and then made a noose from the other which he slipped under his arms. 'C'mon. Get me down there.' He slipped the line securely round a spare cleat and handed the end to Noodles.

'You're joking...'

'Do I look like I am?' he muttered, starting to swing both legs over the fly rail to sit on it.

Noodles took the strain and slowly lowered Rob to where the girl was hanging.

At its full extent the Tallescope reached to just over twenty-five feet, so the injured "fly man" was out of Foz's reach so he took a chance and stood on the rungs of the cradle.

'Still can't get her, Rob.'

'Nearly there. Bit more Noodles.' He descended slowly towards the suspended body.

'Tam's on his way up there,' assured Foz, 'Noodles won't have all your weight.'

'Aye, I'm here,' the Scots voice came from above. 'Y' nearly there?'

Rob drew level with the girl's ankle and checked that the noose holding her in place was not going to slip. After a quick examination he raised his head to the fly floor: 'Tam, drop me a rope asap. Noodles, tie-off.' He didn't trust the way the line was looped and feared that if he lifted the girl the knot would loosen.

'What's going on? said a Welsh voice from below.

He looked down to see the REAG electrician looking up.

'You can't...' started the voice.

'If you quote health and safety at me *once more* I shall form a queue when I get down from here and personally fucking lamp you!'

'But..' the voice died away slightly before, 'I'll ring the emergency services.'

Once the spare line had been dropped to his level, Rob passed it quickly under the girl's arms and tied it off, perhaps tighter than he should have because she moaned, and asked Tam to take up the slack.

'Okay, you're going to get all the weight in a second. Noodles'll have to help.'

As the girl was lifted from being head down to being upright, Rob undid the loop of rope from her ankle and adjusted his position so as to help.

Once the girl was parallel to Rob he grabbed her around the waist and shouted up to the fly floor: 'Nice and gentle, let us both in. Okay?'

'Okay,' the chorus came back.

It was a jerky descent to the stage, but the lines held and soon the girl, now stirring, was laid on the stage.

Cast, musicians and dancers applauded just as a paramedic team wheeled their gurney onto stage, closely followed by a fireman.

Rob sat cross-legged on the stage, his heart thumping and feeling slightly out of breath.

One of the paramedics knelt down beside him: 'Getting on a bit for acrobatics, eh?' he smiled.

'I'm okay. A large brandy would be good though.' From somewhere outside the circle of performers a hip flask was passed to him. He drank deeply.

Rather timidly, Alain called for a break in proceedings.

'Erm...?'

'What is it, Pendry?' sighed Rob, who until that moment had been alone on stage.

'I'm sorry about before, but...'

'I know. Just doing your job. No doubt there'll be a million forms to fill and some pompous bloke in a bowler hat to placate?'

'Well... actually... no.' the voice lilted, 'Front of house don't want... a fuss. So can we just say she fell over?'

Rob eyed the Welshman closely: 'Fell? Over?'

'Erm…'

'If she'll come back and work I'll see what she says. If not, you'd better tell your lot to get the cheque book out – or better still, cash.'

'But…'

'If I went around this place with an H and S bod, and without looking too closely, they'd shut you down before you had time to say "Par Can"… I'm sure you know what I mean?'

The man just nodded and headed back down to his darkened position, front of house, in the stalls.

Noodles, grinning, stepped out from behind one of the black masking legs. 'You didn't lamp him then?'

Rob shook his head and rubbed his underarms where the rope had chafed.

There was a slight pause before Noodles stuck out his hand. 'Thanks, mate. Thanks for…'

'Bollocks. Remember the phrase?'

'Shit happens?'

'Shit happens.'

Rob took the proffered hand and shook it warmly.

The nurse recognised Rob straight away: 'Mister Crowther, isn't it?'

Rob nodded.

'Come to see your mother?'

Several glances were passed between Tam, Noodles, Dickie and Harley.

'Actually, no. One of our workmates had an accident this afternoon. Simmy…'

'Phipps' Noodles remembered.

'Ah, Miss Phipps. Yes. Room 2B. But you can't all pile in there,' stated the nurse looking at the somewhat dishevelled crew. 'Only two visitors at a time.'

As they made their way along the linoleum covered corridor Noodles asked: 'What's that about your mother I thought she was… y'know…?'

'She is, mate. It's just the next door neighbour. Long story,' Rob explained as he pushed open the door to find Simmy sitting up in bed, headphones on, staring at a television.

She smiled as they entered and pulled the earpieces from her head: 'Hi guys,' she smiled, 'that was a bit scary.' she waved at the other crew who were hovering at the threshold.

'How you doing?' asked Noodles.

'Bit sore. Bump on my head and I'll have a scar on my ankle.'

'What happened?' asked Rob.

'I've been thinking about that, and you know what? I don't really know.'

'Meaning?' Noodles cocked his head for the reply.

'Well I took out the cave flat and then went to slacken the brail on the LX. All of a sudden there was a shower of dust; I felt dizzy; saw two red lights and ended up in an ambulance.'

'Two red lights?' Rob queried, 'What? From the rig you mean?'

'No. Right beside me…'

'Like the "eyes of a shit-house rat"' Rob quoted.

Three blue, orb-like lights flitted across the stage and then flew up into the fly floor where they paused for a moment on the rail, and then hovered beside a cleat.

'You know this floor better than we do Harry. What do you think happened?'

'*Can't rightly say, Ma'am.*'

'*Come on, old boy, surely you can make a guess?*'

'*Don't be a bully, Bertie.*'

'*Sorry, Ma'ma.*'

'*Can you make an educated guess Harry?*'

One of the lights separated from the group and span around several cleats and ropes before returning.

'*Lot of dust. Stone dust. And a... a feeling.*'

'*Almost an evil presence?*' suggested Her Ladyship.

'*Aye.*' was the curt reply.

'*You see Bertie, it's not just me who feels it.*'

'*No ma'ma.*'

'*Harry I want everyone to be alerted to this... this presence. I need to know who or what it is before more people get hurt or, God forbid, killed.*'

'*Yes, Ma'am.*'

Rob took his farewell of the girl and the crew and made his way to the ward that lay across the corridor from the lifts on the same floor. He wished that he'd brought some flowers.

Pushing open the door he peered around it and saw the old lady sleeping. He didn't want to disturb her and tried to close the door as quietly as possible, but the self-closer squeaked as he did so.

'Not coming in, Rob?' asked Lil, not opening her eyes.

'Sorry Lil, I thought you were asleep.'

'No, just having a meditate.'

'How are you?' he asked, approaching the bed and pulling up the bedside armchair.

'Hmm. Okay but... y'know...'

'No, I don't. Tell me?'

The old lady opened one eye and stared at Rob for a moment.

He awkwardly shuffled his feet and cleared his throat.

She gave a wry smile. 'Pancreatic cancer.'

'Wh..!'

'It's all right,' she reassured him, 'Hell, when you get to my age you expect… erm…'

'"Shit happens?".' Rob asked.

She chuckled: 'Yes. As you say.' she coughed once and the eye closed.

Rob sat for a moment or two and the silence was deafening. 'Lil?'

The eye opened: 'I've not gone yet, Crowther.' Her face split into a grin. 'I've got your mobile number. I'll let you know.'

It was ten o'clock and the rehearsal was well under way. Rob had dashed up to the fly floor to drop in the necessary pieces at the start of the day and the cast were in buoyant mood. The director was happy and he had expressed his thanks to those involved in yesterdays "mishap". Another round of applause from the cast.

'You'll be getting an Olivier soon,' grinned Dickie.

After a quick break at eleven Alain wanted to go over the part of the script that involved the cave scene – again. He had already cut some dialogue and wanted to make the dancers more "visible".

'We could always ask'm tae git theer tits oot?' suggested Tam, regarding the skeleton-painted bodysuits that the girls were wearing.

'Wouldn't work, Mate,' Harley idly suggested.

'An' why no'?'

'There'd be too many "boners" on side of stage,' he grinned.

Alain rose from his seat on the forestage. 'Let's do this again. I want to get the change from outer to inner as smooth as possible.'

'Bollocks,' stated Rob, 'I'll dive up the fly floor,' he stated, wearily

Noodles placed a hand on Rob's arm: 'Had y' passion.'

'Eh?'

'Oh, Flys?' said the tech manager looking up.

'What y' effin want?' came back the reply.

'STEVIE!' was the shouted chorus from Rob, Tam and Dickie.

'What? Proper effin flyman up here now!'

'When did you get him?' Rob asked Noodles.

'Made a call after we'd been to the hospital.'

'May I?' Rob asked, holding a hand towards the gallery.

'Be my guest.' Noodles grinned back.

Rob looked into the gloom of the roof. 'If you fall off there don't expect me to come and rescue you, and I am definitely not giving you the kiss of life, y' hairy arsed bastard.'

'Eff off!' came back the light-hearted reply.

'You alright up there?'

'No I'm effin not!'

'Whatsup?'

'Th's no effin porn. Just this shite.' A fluttering from above descended to the stage and Rob crossed to pick up what was a magazine. It was "Rock Climbing Monthly".

He laughed out loud and threw the publication across to Dickie.

'That's theatre, luvvie,' he commented.

'If we're all quite finished..?' Alain complained.

'Sorry Alain,' apologised Rob, 'Old friend.'

The director nodded. 'If we can continue..?'

'Sorry…'

'Sam, if you would call the dancers please?' Alain instructed.

From the prompt desk, the DSM depressed the Tannoy button and made the call backstage for the rest of the dancers to be ready in their costume and to attend the stage.

There was suddenly a flurry of activity as a couple of skeleton-body-suited dancers, together with six of the Babes, pushed through the on-stage door, from upstage left, and then a scream and a thud.

'Oh, what friggin' now!' exclaimed Alain.

One of the babes screamed.

Noodles and Rob were there in an instant.

Lying in the off stage corridor at the bottom of the stairs leading to the dressing rooms was a dancer that they knew as "Zilly" – so named because she'd had breast implants and someone had said it looked like a view down Silicone Valley – there was a slight gash on her head and she was holding her left leg.

'What happened?' asked Alain, joining the two stage techies.

'I... I... I don't...' she sobbed, 'I tripped in some dust.'

'Dust?' repeated the incredulous director.

'It was dust and red,' blurted the girl.

'We'll help her back to the dressing room,' Rob stated, stepping forward to hold open the door.

He and Noodles picked up the damaged dancer between them and climbed the stairs to dressing room eight. "Twirley Haven" it stated on the door.

They placed the girl on a chaise longue and Noodles asked if she felt any better.

'Not really,' she admitted, 'feels like I've twisted something.'

'Ambulance or taxi?' suggested Rob.

'Sorry,' the girl apologised, 'taxi, please'

'While Noodles rang a local cab firm Rob crouched down beside the girl: 'When you said you tripped in some dust and saw red, what did you mean?'

'Well...' she considered for a moment, 'I was coming down the stairs – the curvy bit by the landing – and all of a sudden there was this flash of red light and a swirl of ... of dust... and I fell down the last flight.'

'Did the red bits look like eyes?' probed Rob.

'I... I don't think so...' she hesitated.'

'Okay. Taxi'll be here soon.'

Whilst the rest of the cast and crew adjourned to the Bodger, Rob made his way to the Circle and sat in the third row back – the best seats in the house.

He had sat silently for a moment before plucking up his courage – or was he just daft, he thought?

'Come out, wherever you are?' he muttered, and then repeated it in a louder voice.

He waited.

'C'mon! Where are you?'

He waited.

'F' fecks sake, … c'mon. Talk to me!' he shouted into the empty auditorium, his voice echoing back at him.

'Should we mama?'

'You know we cannot, Bertie.'

'But we may be able to help?'

'Not at present.'

'Hmm…'

After an half hour of sitting in the plush-covered seat, Rob wearily got to his feet and as he did so his mobile phone beeped that he had received a message. He flipped open the cover. "1 week left," read the text message. It was from Lil. A lump grew in his throat and he frantically suppressed the tears in his eyes.

The performance area had been swept and washed, the carpet runners were hoovered and now the full cast, in costume, assembled centre stage for their ten o'clock call.

The production team had moved into the auditorium for Act Two.

A sheet of eight feet by four feet plywood, painted black, had been placed across several seats in rows three and four, and hold a small reading lamp.

Flynn, Alain and Dan sat drinking coffee – not of the crew room variety – in row five and the musicians warmed up in the pit.

The crew, apart from Stevie, waited in the wings.

Sam stepped from her position at the prompt desk to signal Alain, with a thumbs-up, that everyone was present.

The director rose from his seat, the padded cushion slamming noisily to the upright position, and made his way to the centre aisle and from there up the stairs at the side of the auditorium and onto the forestage.

'Good morning, everyone,' he greeted, 'first of all some news. You will be pleased to know that Zilly's fall was not as serious as we first thought. She's got the morning off and will rejoin us this afternoon.'

Appreciative smiles and sighs of relief spread through the cast.

'Secondly,' he continued, 'Simmy will not be our fly person on this show as she's been told to keep off her injured ankle. Our flyman will be Stevie.' He gestured towards the fly floor.

A grunt was heard from above.

'Never one for elaborate greetings,' remarked Dickie, looking flywards.

'I would all like you to be aware, stated the director, 'that the stage and its environs can be dangerous, so please take the utmost care whether you are on it, above it or below it. Now, let's get on with it. I'd like to finish by four so that everyone can have a break before the first show.'

'Stevie!' shouted Noodles, 'I'll let the break go down here for the tabs. You want to lock on?'

'Yeah. Will do,' came back the short reply from above.

'Fifteen minutes everyone, please.' Sam stated in a raised voice, 'Fifteen to beginners.'

'Any last jobs?' asked Noodles to Rob.

'Cyc needs stretching,' Rob answered, nodding to the cloth upstage. 'Apart from that...' he shrugged.

'I'll get it,' stated Foz.

'We'll do a brew. Tea or coffee?'

'Coffee – as long as it's the proper kind.'

Leaving Foz to deal with short battens of timber, butterfly bolts and sashcord, which would be tied off to the walls from the cyclorama cloth to stretch it tight, the rest of the team adjourned to the crew room.

'Anyone going for a tab?' asked Dickie.

'Yeah, why not. The tea'll still be hot – drinkable – when we get back,' said Rob.

They made their way down the flight of stairs to the stage door and went out into the street.

'You alright, Rob? asked the techie pulling at his goatee, once the cigarettes had been lit.

'Yeah, mate. Why'd you ask?'

'You just seem a bit... y'know... preoccupied?'

Rob exhaled a long stream of smoke which was whisked away by the wind that whipped down the street: 'Nah... I'm okay... just...'

'Preoccupied?' offered Dickie.

Rob paused before answering: 'How long have we known each other, Dickie?'

'Shit! I don't know? Twenty years?'

'In all that time would you describe me as "weird"?'

'Weird? Naah! If I'd say anything I'd it'd be that if you had enough money you'd be described as *eccentric*.' he grinned.

Rob chuckled.

'You've always led from the front, Rob. You wouldn't expect anyone to do anything that you weren't willing to have a go at yourself.'

'Thanks, Dickie.'

The man shrugged. 'It's true, though.' He took a deep drag on his cigarette.

'So, if I told you that Tam and Foz have always reckoned that there's ghosts in the theatre, and that I think that I've seen them, you wouldn't be surprised?'

'Blue lights? Go straight through you? Coldness?' Nah.'

Rob nodded and then flicked his dog end towards a drain. 'I think it's the ghosts that are causing all this shit with the panto,' he stated.

The techie raised an eyebrow, flicked the remains of his own cigarette towards the drain and said, 'Can't be. Everyone has said that it's sort of dusty and red.'

'True.'

'Can't be ghosts. C'mon, I'm getting cold and there's tea waiting.'

'I *do not believe* that Welsh twat!' Foz's raised voice was evident to all those assembled in the crewroom before he entered.

'Problem?' Noodles asked.

'Hah! Stupid Celtic cu… twat… says I've got to sign a chitty before I can climb a ladder to do the cyc!'

'What?' Rob replied, incredulous.

'If I want to stretch off the cyc I've got to sign a form to say that all the H and S requirements have been met,' Foz fumed.

Noodles was on his feet. 'Leave it to me.'

'Stand by fly cue twenty-one; LX cues thirty-two and three; Sound cue nineteen;' ordered Sam over the headsets.

The replies came back.

'Standing by.'

'Standing by.'

'Standing by.'

The cue light in the orchestra pit flashed red, was acknowledged, and turned green.

The musicians reprised the overture and at the sound of the gong

Sam gave the fly cue.

At this point the front of house curtain was supposed to fly out to reveal the busy, updated, laundry of the Widow Twankey. Nothing happened.

'Flys?' asked the girl, 'Flys?'

'Not a effin thing!' came back the strained voice of Stevie, 'Some effin twat's put the brake on down on stage.'

The music petered out in the pit.

The girl turned to Noodles who was hovering near to the prompt desk: 'The stage brake's been left on.'

Noodles dashed across stage, through the actors and dancers, towards the stage right where there was a supplementary brake for the fly floor to operate the tabs. It was securely chained off into the "open" position.

He moved into line of sight and held out his open arms and shrugged across to Sam.

'Stevie? It's off.'

'Bollocks! Something's effin stuck then!'

'Stevie!' shouted Rob, who had been keeping a weather eye on proceedings, 'Nip up the rail and see if the cradle rail's okay'

'On me effin way!' came the irritated reply from above.

Moments later there was another shout from above: 'Nowt!'

'What is it, Stevie?' Rob asked.

'Some effin fuckwit' chained off the effin cradle down there, I think!'

'Chained it off…?' asked Noodles incredulously.

'What I effin said. Chained it off.'

'Can you get it undone?' asked the tech manager.

Rob scrambled over the cage that held the flying machinery and up to the weight-cradle that counterbalanced the flying bar and was some twenty-odd feet above the stage level.

'Shackles a bit … tight… Okay. Chain's off.'

There was the sound of metal upon metal as Rob withdrew the

chain that had been holding the counterweight cradle securely to the flying channels.

'Should be okay,' he shouted up to the fly floor.

'Give it a bounce!' instructed Noodles.

'Two effin secs. I've got to get there!'

Suddenly the front of house curtain rose out, at speed, and was then brought back in again only to be taken back out.

'Effin lush!' said the voice from the fly floor.

'Tabs in please, Stevie.' instructed Noodles.

Sam stepped to the fore and shouted; 'Stand by on stage!' as the curtain gently descended.

'I see we got the cyc stretched.' Rob noted to Noodles as he jumped down from the fly cage. 'Have a word with Pendry, did you?'

'Nah. Didn't need to,' he grinned, 'I just got some bits of paper and wrote "Condemned" on them before fastening them to all his ladders with hazard tape.'

'Strange that.'

'Hnn… Cyc's stretched out quite nicely.'

'Excuse me mama.'

'What is it, Bertie? I'm trying to watch the rehearsal.'

'I believe that Harry has found out what has happened.'

'Yes?'

'He-he! Rosencrantz and Guildenstern are not dead.'

'Jeez, I'm sick of eating bloody burgers!' exclaimed Rob, throwing the remains of his evening meal into the large dustbin that hogged a corner of the crew room. 'It tastes like minced shite with lettuce in a piece of cardboard.'

'Ah, the joys of fast food,' grinned Harley as he tucked into a breaded chicken leg.

'Least it's not Spam,' offered Foz, 'I've been doing a lot of that lately since our lass left.'

Dickie grinned, evilly: 'What? Soft Porn *And* Masturbation?'

His reply was the crust of a cheese and coleslaw sandwich thrown at his head.

The Tannoy crackled with Sam's voice: 'Ladies and gentlemen, this is your fifteen minute call.'

'Bollocks!' uttered Tam, knowing that they had twenty minutes until the show started, and rolling himself a cigarette,

'Everything alright your end?' asked Noodles, aside.

'Seems to be,' replied Rob, 'just hope we don't have any major fuck-ups.'

'Going for a ciggy?'

Rob nodded, rose to his feet and followed Noodles to the stage door where several members of the cast, in costume, were assembled taking a last shot of nicotine before the show.

As Noodles and Rob smoked quietly in the dark street, lit at intervals by sallow puddles of orange sodium, Paul Bigg, was standing in a domestic doorway adjacent to the stage door. He was grinning, and commented, 'I hope there's no paparazzi lurking, Sonna.'

'Why's that?' asked Rob.

'Well... can you not see it on the culture pages of the "Guardian"? Shots of Panto stars having a quick drag before going on stage?' at which point he farted, loudly. 'Better out than in,' he observed.

'I do hope the resident of that flat's not in, Paul,' stated Noodles.

The actor gave a wry grin. 'Why's that?'

'Coz you just rattled his letterbox with last night's tea...'

'Sweet as a nut!' he interjected.

From the top of the stairs that lead to the stage someone shouted, "Five!"

Three of the dancers, shivering in tightly wrapped pink towelling robes, flicked their cigarette butts towards a drain.

'Always the same,' grumbled one, who Rob thought was called Emily, 'It's the shortest fag break ever. Fifteen turns to five in three minutes.' And with that pearl of pre-performance wisdom the trio made their way back through the stage door.

'I hope this goes okay,' muttered Noodles, gazing wistfully at the last of his cigarette. 'First one. Don't want any more accidents.'

'It'll be fine,' reassured Rob. 'You keep your eyes open and so will I.'

In the Stalls Bar everyone had been served with whatever drink they needed and groups of cast, now in "civvies", were chatting and laughing as the stage crew entered from the pass door after doing the set-back.

'First one out of the way and only another forty-eight to do,' Harley stated.

'Aye. Three back-to-back t'morrow,' Tam stated, 'That'll be fun. Not.'

'What else would you be doing on a Saturday?' grinned Dickie sidling up to the counter.

'What's the call?' Foz asked Rob.

'Noodles? Call tomorrow?' enquired Rob, passing the message on.

'We'd better make it nine.'

A glass being pinged alerted them to the director taking centre stage for his post show chat.

'Ladies and gentlemen…' he tapped the wine glass again with a pen. 'Cast and crew and other members, if I may…'

Silence descended in an end of conversation trickle.

Alain raised his glass and said: 'Cheers.' before taking a sip, 'Thank you everyone for your hard work and for your patience with the last minute changes to what was written in the script. I don't intend to do an autopsy this evening as I need to speak to Flynn – who has some further changes, I'm afraid – but I need to say that I want everyone on stage at eleven tomorrow morning to do a run-through of some sticky bits.'

Some of the cast's smiles flattened.

'Bugger!' Noodles said as an aside, 'That only gives us a couple of hours.'

'There's not that much to do,' Rob observed.

'I noticed the cave entrance flattage was leaning a bit,' answered Noodles, 'I need to tighten up the lines.

Rob nodded. He, too, had noticed the scenery sagging. 'That'll not take long.'

'Not a bad show, mama.'

'Not the worst I've seen, Bertie. Is Julius going to join us?'

'I did ask pre-show but you know what he's like?'

'Indeed. But if, as you say, Rosencrantz and Guildenstern are not dead then we need to inform Mister Crowther as to what is occurring.

'You mean actually tell him? Face to face?'

'Do you envisage any other way of informing him?'

'Well…erm…'

'Don't tell me that Julius is still afraid to come out of the lavatory?'

'He's… er… apprehensive, shall we say.'

'Oh, for goodness sake! I shall have to speak to him.'

'Yes Mama.'

'Yes I do know how late it is but I've been at work and it's the only time that I can see her,' Rob cajoled the ward sister. 'I'm like you lot. Work stupid hours.' He had been feeling very guilty about not visiting Lil for two days and had diverted the taxi cab towards the hospital instead of going straight home after the show.

'I'll see if she's awake,' scolded the nurse.

Rob waited in the corridor for approval to see his neighbour, before being waved towards the room.

'Two minutes, Mister Crowther,' warned the sister, 'she's very tired.'

Rob nodded and sidled past the uniform into Lil's room.

'First night, Robert?' asked the old lady.

Rob nodded.

'How did it go?'

He spent the next ten minutes explaining the shows ups, downs and in and outs.

A female voice cleared its throat at the door: 'Erm...' the nurse tapped her watch.

'Sorry, Lil,' he shrugged, 'they're clock watching.'

'Never mind. You take care and I'll text you,' she nodded.

He stroked her hand before getting up from the chair: 'Anything I can get you?'

'Christmas?' she suggested, before slowly closing her eyes.

Even though he'd enjoyed a *very* large brandy – with a cigar – before bed, after checking the pile of post behind Lil's front door, Rob had a very restless night.

He had woken at one point with the image of a skeletal Santa Claus riding off in a sleigh, pulled by equally skeletal reindeer, with Lil reaching out towards him.

He had finally risen at six and had pottered aimlessly around the empty house for a couple of hours before calling a cab to take him to work.

Tom was in the middle of filling the kettle as he entered the stage door.

'Hmm... what'd you do?' asked the doorman, 'wet the bed?' he grinned.

'First in, I guess?' Rob stated.

His answer was a nod.

'Tea?' Tom enquired holding up a mug.

'Nah. I'll get one in the crew room. I'm going for a piss.'

Tom, with a sly grin said: 'Give me a shout if you need a hand... or two...'

Rob made his way up the ramp from stage door, through the on-stage door, across stage past the props tables, through the off stage door on prompt side and down the corridor to the toilet.

He was mid-stream when he thought he heard a whispered voice from the direction of the cistern above his head.

'Robert?'

'Wha'?'

'Robert. I need a word.'

Rob suddenly realised that he was urinating onto his boot and quickly diverted back to the sani-block that he had been trying to flush towards the drain.

'Mister Julius?' asked Rob, in nervous disbelief.

'Yes Robert.'

'Whoa!' he exclaimed. His ablutions stopped and he shook and zipped as fast as he could before running from the toilet.

With an unsteady hand he made a strong cup of tea and fifteen minutes later, as he was draining the mug, Dickie entered the crew room.

'Mornin' Rob,' he greeted, 'all set for another day of ...' he paused.

'You alright, mate? You look like you've seen a ghost?'

'Heard one,' Rob stated.

Dickie cocked his head: 'Heard one?'

'Remember Julius?' Rob asked referring to a former operations manager of the theatre that had been electrocuted in the toilet.

'Couldn't not forget him.' Dickie stated.

'About ten minutes ago I heard him in the bog.'

'Fuck off.'

'I'm telling you. Ten or so minutes ago I went for a piss and the bugger called my name.'

'You still rat-arsed from last night?'

Rob shook his head. 'He called my name and said he needed a word.'

'What did you do?'

'What the fuck d' think I did? I got out of there – pronto.'

'The lads'll love this,' Dickie stated, switching on the kettle.

'Don't you fucking dare!' Rob slammed his empty mug down next to the singing kettle. 'The last thing I need is the piss taken.'

Dickie nodded sagely: 'Okay I'll not say anything,' adding, 'was that supposed to be a pun?'

'Bowlines do not untie themselves!' exclaimed Noodles observing the two slack ropes that dangled next to their tie-off points on the cave entrance flattage. 'Some bastard is trying to sabotage this bleedin' show!'

'Pendry!' shouted Rob.

The in-house electrician's head appeared from behind his lighting desk at the back of the stalls: 'Yes?'

'Who'd you think would want to sabotage this show?' Rob asked, point blank.

The man just shrugged: 'Don't see that anyone would. Not from REAG.'

'What's the chance of getting a night-man in here?'

'None. Unless you pay for it.' He ducked back down behind the desk.

'Bollocks!' exclaimed Noodles bending down to re-tie the knots. 'We'll have to do a sneaky.'

'A sneaky?' asked Rob.

'You and me. Nightshift?'

'On the Q T?'

The tech manager nodded twice.

'Three shows and then an all-nighter..?'

'You got a better suggestion?'

'So Julius failed to speak to Mister Crowther. Is that what you're telling me?'

'Sorry, Mama, yes.'

'Oh, that man!'

'Yes Mama.'

'If you want something done, Bertie, then it's best to do it yourself. Now how can we get Mister Crowther into the lift?'

There had only been one instance of panic during the three Saturday shows and that was when one of the pyros at the front of stage had, inexplicably, set off the other three and the gerb flare obscuring Abanazer in a voluminous cloud of smoke and sparks then leaving him to "appear" throughout the rest of the first act without the dramatic effect of the fireworks.

'Take him up slowly on the trap. Like he's rising through the floor,' had come the instruction from Alain via Sam to get around the absence of the effects.

The slight diversion with Tom and Pendry had worked. Rob and Noodles had made an excuse to go back into the theatre, from the pub, and Noodles had returned the keys with the tale that he and Rob were going to share a cab home and that it was pending. Noodles had snuck back into the stage door where Rob was waiting.

'Front or on?' asked Noodles, referring to sitting either in the auditorium or on stage.

'Let's take turns,' suggested Rob, 'an hour in each.'

'Front or on?' repeated Noodles.

'I'll do "on" for the first shift. Okay?'

The tech manager merely nodded and used the pass door to access the auditorium.

Rob listened to the creaks and groans of the theatre cooling down but didn't notice anything suspicious on stage as he sat on the prompt desk high-chair. Nothing.

'Ready to swap?' asked a voice behind him.

Rob jumped and stood up in such a panic that the chair tipped over.

'Christ! Don't sneak up on me like that.'

Noodles grinned. 'Sorry mate.'

As Noodles took up his position at the prompt desk, Rob made his way front of house towards the wide sweeping staircase.

He was only three treads up when the small foyer lift light came on and the door rattled. He shuddered.

'Hello?' he asked with anticipation.

With no reply forthcoming he descended the stairs and went to the lift gate to check it. The lift had been installed in the 1920s and was far from reliable – he knew that it had crashed down three floors when overloaded on one occasion killing a local dignitary, her son and the lift boy.

'Hello?' he repeated, drawing aside the steel gate and stepping inside.

The gate slammed shut behind him and the motor sprang into life.

Immediately he was at the control panel and was pressing buttons. Stalls. Circle. Upper. Gods. Stop. Emergency. Nothing worked.

Between the Circle and the Upper Circle the lift shuddered to a halt and the lights flickered for a moment.

When the illumination returned Rob hurredly and with some trepidation, looked around the car. There on the mirror that backed the lift was a message written onto what was now icily-frosted glass: "*Rosencrantz and Guildenstern are not dead!*"

'I'm telling you it was written on the mirror!' exclaimed Rob, having managed to leave the lift at Upper Circle level and made his way back down to the stage to grab Noodles and bring him to the lift to show him what was written.

'"Rosencrantz and Guildenstern are not dead". That's what was written?' asked Noodles, rubbing at what was now a plain mirror.

'Yes!' Rob stated categorically.

Noodles pondered for a moment: 'Okay. Hamlet. Two guys – who are the king's men – out to trap the prince?'

Rob nodded. 'Who get sent off and don't come back.'

'Tom Stoppard production of the same name?'

Rob nodded again.

'Anything else?'

Rob shrugged.

'Let's have a cuppa and think about this one,' Noodles suggested.

The bistro was half full when Rob and Noodles entered it at ten minutes to nine on the Sunday morning. It had opened at eight-thirty for the market traders, whose stalls opened at ten.

'Two double cappuccinos and two large brandies,' ordered Rob, bleary eyed.

As they sat at the small table next to the door they savoured the strong coffee and their thoughts.

It was Noodles who broke their silence. 'So, nothing.'

Rob shook his head. 'Doesn't look like it. No spooks but a message.'

'You're sure that "Rosencrantz and Guildenstern are not dead" means nothing to you?'

'I keep telling you. Apart from Shakespeare and Stoppard, nothing.'

The silence resumed.

At ten o'clock, after calling into the local burger bar down the road for an all day breakfast, they walked back to the stage door. Half way there it started to sleet and Rob looked up at the grey sky. 'Bugger! It'll be snow by tea-time and we'll...' he stopped abruptly in his tracks and his gaze shifted to the roof of the theatre.

'What?' asked Noodles, looking up.

Rob pointed to the apex of the theatre façade. 'Rosencrantz and Guildenstern.'

'Eh?'

'Y' see the two statues holding the vase?'

'The dirty looking angel things?'

'Rosencrantz and Guildenstern. Or rather, Ravenscrap and Goldenstern.'

'What?'

'When the theatre was built those two… thingys… were donated by one of the patrons. He said they were a gift to decorate the roof and were put into place about a month or so after the place opened.'

'So?'

'From what I remember they are two angel-shaped bits of stone – they're mirrored in the cartouches on the front of the circle and what-have-you. They are holding onto the vase that have the tragic-comedy masks on it. When the builders put them in place, one of them said they were "Rosencrantz and Guildenstern" but they were re-christened when one of them got shit on by, I presume, a raven.'

'What about Goldenstern?'

Rob shrugged and pulled up his collar against the heavier sleet.

'"Rosencrantz and Guildenstern are not dead" was what you saw. What the fuck does that mean?'

'I don't know, Mate, but I aim to find out.' Rob shucked his blouson jacket and headed for the stage door.

'Asleep on the job!' exclaimed Foz as he entered the crew room with Dickie and Tam, and woke both Rob and Noodles.

'Party animals,' Tam responded, with a wry grin.

Noodles stood and stretched. 'I wish. Put the kettle on,' he yawned as he spoke.

'Eleven and two,' stated Harley as he joined them, referring to the day's performances. 'Means we get to go to the pub between-times.'

Rob just groaned and Noodles wiped the sleep from his eyes.

'Flippin' heck!' exclaimed Dickie, 'What a pair of decrepit bastards,' he mocked. 'Three shows and you're knackered.'

Rob stuck up two fingers in the general direction of the comment, with a grimace.

Once they were all seated with steaming cups of coffee or tea, Noodles stood up and shut the crew room door: 'Where's Pendry?' he asked.

'He's no' in yet,' Tam stated.

'Good. Let me tell you what's going on.'

At the end of half an hour Noodles had recounted the previous evening's escapades and the subsequent solving of the Hamlet reference.

Foz and Tam nudged each other at the mention of a ghost with an "I told you so" look.

'So what you're trying to tell us is that two statues from the roof of the building are responsible for the fuck-ups that have happened?' Dickie shook his head, his incredulity apparent.

Both Rob and Noodles nodded.

'Bollocks!' stated Tam sipping his coffee. 'Ah c'n ken th' ghosties but a couple o' statues comin' t' life..?'

'That's why, between shows, I want us to go up to the roof,' Rob announced.

'It's pissing down with snow, in case you hadn't noticed,' replied Foz.

There was a thud against the door and then a loud knock: 'Stop effin shaggin' and let us in!' exclaimed Stevie's voice from the other side.

'So how'd you want to do this?' Noodles asked.

'Just ask the old bugger to go for a ciggie. Whilst you're out on the street I'll get the key to the roof from the cabinet and off we go,' explained Rob.

'What if he won't go?'

'He will. Just… wiggle your arse … or something…'

'Thanks,' Noodles grinned in response.

'Frickin hell, I didn't remember these many stairs,' complained Rob, pausing for breath and holding his sides, as they scaled the back stairs of the Gods.

'Not far to go,' Noodles wheezed, also pausing.

They climbed the remaining two flights and pushed open the anonymous door at the top, to find a further small entrance accessed via two stone steps.

Rob rattled the key, on its fob, in his hand.

'Let's see what the Hamlets have to say,' he muttered as he turned the key in the lock and pushed open the door, which was stiff with age.

Ahead of them the roof was a plain of white, the snow coming down at a sixty degree angle, eddying slightly in the chill wind.

Stepping onto the virgin snow they approached the rear of the statues, which sat apparently holding on to the ornamental vase, on the apex of the theatre façade. Noodles ran his hand down the one on the left, brushing the snow from it.

Rob patted the right hand side figure on the rump and then tested its stability by grabbing hold of the square-cut wings and trying to move it from its plinth.

'Which one's which?' asked Noodles.

'Buggered if I know,' admitted Rob, stepping back. 'Looks like I could have been wrong.'

'Funny looking things ain't they?' Noodles observed after leaning over the wall for a better look at the front of the carvings.

'Eh?'

'Well with the square-cut wings and the side-on feet they look a bit... sort of...'

'Egyptian?' Rob suggested.

Noodles nodded.

As the two men locked the door behind them to return to the stage, the figure that Rob had tested shuddered its wings and a feint red light glowed in its eye sockets.

'That did not go as well as I expected'

'Mama?'

'Mister Crowther looking at the statues.'

'It's probably because of the cold. Snow y'know.'

'Yes Bertie, I have seen the inclement precipitation.'

'Mama?'

'I was wondering if any of the others could help in any way to alert Mister Crowther to the situation.'

'Should I call a full meeting?'

'Hmm... Yes Bertie. I think that may be wise.'

Monday was a day off so Rob stayed in bed until ten and then luxuriated in the bath for over an hour.

Padding around the house in nothing but a towling robe he flicked the dust from the most obvious places with an ancient duster and ran the vacuum cleaner a quick circuit of the carpets downstairs.

Realising that he had done his morning chores in reverse order he quickly jumped into the shower before dressing. The bath had been a luxury; the shower a necessity.

Just after noon he nuked a chilli con carne in the microwave and then set off for the local library; he needed to know about the two figures on top of the theatre and the local history section would be the place to find it.

Finding nothing of relevance in local books he had asked the attendant and ascertained that the internet computers were for the use of library members only, and had been given a day pass to use them. It was getting dark outside before he found what he was looking for.

Returning home via the corner shop to stock up on milk and bread, he again made use of the microwave – a Tagliatelli this time – before ringing Noodles.

'Guess what?' Rob opened the conversation.

'Oh… I don't know… The Pope's Jewish and the Queen's your auntie?' Noodles replied facetiously.

'Close, but no cigar,' grinned Rob, 'The two statues?'

'Uh-ha?'

'They're not Egyptian, they're Persian. Very old and they were donated by a benefactor who had done the equivalent of the Grand Tour.'

'Right..?'

'Seems he nicked them from some temple; shipped them back; donated them.'

'And the point being?'

'Later in life he reckoned that they'd brought him nothing but bad luck and so that's why he got rid of them. Said they sometimes had red eyes.'

'Mister Mitchell you were there when they topped out the building and had your unfortunate accident.'

'I was, your Ladyship, but them things weren't added 'til later.'

'Does anyone remember when they were installed?'

'Doesn't look like it, Mama.'

'Mister Thomas you were around at that time? Do you not remember?'

One of the blue lights that had assembled in the Gods Bar peeked out from behind another: 'Brought in outsiders to put 'em in. Lads didn't like them at the time. Still don't. Later on not even the Luftwaffe could shift 'em. Bomb went off down in the street and those two buggers – pardon language – just sat there. Though one did get damaged and got repaired with concrete.'

'We need to get Mister Crowther to realise that one, or perhaps both, have been…'

'Activated?' suggested Bertie.

'Yes, activated. By what and by whom I don't know but we all shall do our utmost to find out.'

Rob was soaked. He had been caught in the downpour on the way from the Metro transit to the stage door. The snow had lasted a week of freezing conditions and was now being washed into the gutters like so much greying Tuesday slush.

'Should've brought your brolly,' observed Tom at the stage door by way of greeting.

'Hindsight is a marvellous thing,' Rob replied, slipping out of his drenched blouson.

'You're last in.' Tom grimaced at the puddle that was forming around Rob. 'Go and take your wet self to the crew room.'

'I thought you liked "wet" men,' Rob threw as a parting gesture.

'Huh! There's "wet" and there's "*wet*".' Tom muttered to Rob's departing back as he reached into the space of a cupboard, behind his desk, for a mop.

The smell of freshly brewed coffee met Rob as he walked up the ramp and turned left, along the short passage, into the crew room.

Tom had been right; he was the last of the crew to arrive.

Over the past week the room had been made slightly more habitable by changing the overhead bulb for a brighter one and a laptop computer had been installed to watch movies between shows. Someone – probably Noodles – had started to get into the Christmas spirit and an artificial tree was propped against the far wall, in a recess, waiting to be assembled and dressed. Above it there was a cut-out newspaper image of Kylie Monogue on which someone had penned the comment, "actual size".

'Mornin'.' Rob greeted the assembly.

Dickie and Foz were watching a subtitled film and hardly glanced at him, but did attempt a wave.

'What you watching?'

'"Black Book".' replied Dickie without looking around.

'Aye. Nazi porn more like.' was Tam's comment.

'Dunno how y' can follow them effin subtitles and watch the film.' Stevie looked up from his Daily Sport newspaper. 'Morning Rob.' his head ducked back down to his study of the female form and his daily nipple count.

'Noodles around?' asked Rob.

'Stage.' replied Harley without looking up from a motorcycle magazine.

Rob hung his drenched coat next to the radiator, grabbed a paper towel from the dispenser to dry off his soaked hair and made his way to the on-stage door.

Scrunching the, now sodden, towel he lobbed it towards a backstage dustbin and it hovered on the rim before falling in.

'Noodles?' shouted Rob.

'Yeah. Prompt desk.' came back the slightly muffled reply from down stage left.

Rather than cross behind the cyc, where the tables held the various props for the pantomime, Rob walked down the OP wing and across the front of stage.

'What you doing?' Rob asked as he approached the desk.

'Oh, not a lot. Contemplating why belly-button fluff is always blue and not looking forward to the writer coming in for more script changes.'

'Flipping heck! More changes? The cast won't know which way is up after last week.'

Noodles nodded: 'That, and cutting half our cues. The comics reckon I could now do it with half a crew.'

'You're not thinking of...'

'Nah! If I cut now I'll not get for next year. Sleeping Beauty with only a couple of crew? I think not.'

'What time is he due?'

'Him, the comics and Alain in about twenty minutes.'

'What about the set back?' asked Rob, referring to the setting up for the first scene of act one.

'Plenty of time. Show's not 'til one and it's only eleven-ish.'

Rob nodded: 'Follow up any of that stuff about the Hamlets?'

'Went to those web sites that you suggested but I think we're okay. Last week went without a hitch – apart from the trap getting stuck on that matinée – so I don't think we've a lot to worry about. Come on, let's have a cuppa.'

The curtain had just gone up on the second act of the first show and Rob was just about to travel down to the traps when the red light started to flash above the prompt desk.

'Fire?' asked Sam.

Rob grabbed the handset from the wall phone and dialled "9". It rang twice before being answered.

'Fire?' asked Rob repeating Sam's unanswered question.

'Panel out here says triggered in the Gods Bar,' replied Aggie, the Front of House manager. 'Someone's checking,' and hung up.

Thirty or so seconds later, the green light flashed on the phone. Rob grabbed it: 'Fire?'

'Looks like a false alarm.'

'Thanks.'

'No evac?' asked Noodles joining Rob at the desk.

'Nope. False alarm.'

The red light started to flash again.

Rob grabbed the phone and repeated the procedure.

Again the answer came back that it was a false alarm.

The third time the light started to flash, so did the green one on the phone.

'Fire?' snatched Rob.

'Do an evac. I can't be sure and I'd rather be safe than sorry,' was Aggie's answer.

'Sam, do a Mister Sands please,' requested Rob, giving her the code word to relay front of house and back stage, over the Tannoy system, for a full evacuation of the theatre.

Without warning the front of house tabs slowly descended and then Noodles went straight to the control panel to release the heavy steel fire curtain that protected stage from the auditorium and vice versa.

Actors and dancers started to stream from the stage towards the exits and Rob and Noodles dashed to dressing rooms to check that they had been vacated. They met on the street a few minutes later.

Tom was taking a roll call from the signing-in sheet that everyone had autographed on their way through his domain. Sirens could be heard approaching the venue.

'Bloody great!' Noodles exclaimed, 'why couldn't we have a fire when it wasn't raining.'

'I'll do it if you want,' Rob offered.

'Yeah. Go on. You've done it before and I'd hate to face my public looking like a washed out dishrag,' replied Alain, still dripping water onto the stage from his enforced time outside.

Rob parted the front of house curtain and stepped out onto the forestage. He'd had the foresight to change into a dry tee-shirt and to slick back his hair.

He entered the space grinning at Alain's pretentious "my public": 'Boys and girls, ladies and gentlemen, we'd like to apologise for the unexpected and unplanned interval to the show and hope that you will bear with us for a few minutes whilst we dry off Aladdin, Wishey Washee and Widow Twankey. They all look like they need wringing out.'

A few of the audience laughed.

'Whilst we're drying off, please take advantage of the bars and café facilities – free coffee – and we will resume in five minutes. Thank you.'

For his short appearance he gained a ripple of applause before passing back behind the tabs.

'Thanks Rob,' said Alain, shaking his hand in gratitude.

'Nowt's the bother,' Rob assured him.

'PUB!' screamed Foz, 'I need beer!'

'He's effin keen,' Stevie observed.

'Yeah, well, with the fire drill we've only got a half hour before the next performance.' replied Dickie.

'PUB!' shouted Stevie, grabbing his coat from the hook above the radiator and throwing it on.

There followed a stampede towards the Bodger by the crew, closely followed by several of the cast.

Rob was already at the bar with Alain, supping a pint of Guinness.

'How'd you get here so effin fast?' asked Stevie.

Rob winked, 'Friends in high places.' He nodded surreptitiously towards the director.

'So you were saying, Rob, that these statues..?' asked Alain.

After the second show, which passed without incident, the crew were again in the pub, but this time assembled round their usual table.

Alain came up to the table with the writer: 'Don't suppose any of you chaps have found a diary?' he asked.

Flynn Forbins was looking decidedly agitated as he hovered next to Noodles. 'All my appointments and notes for the last year…' he explained.

The general consensus was that no-one had seen a diary anywhere.

After they had left, Rob whispered to Noodles to join him in the toilet.

His reply was a nod.

'Ghosts' stated Rob as Noodles entered the lavatory.

'Ghosts?'

'They've nicked his diary and we just have to find it.'

'Piss off… you've had one too many "Nigerians".'

'Bet?' Rob held out an open palm that the tech manager just stared at.

'You've managed to secure some information for Mister Crowther, I understand?'

'Yes y'ur Ladyship.'

'Well done Mister Mitchell. I trust that you will leave it in a suitable position for him to find?'

'I thought I may ask Mister Julius to … erm … drop it in his lap, so to speak.'

'Doing anything nice for Christmas, Professor?' asked his secretary as the learned man was about to depart for his holiday.

He turned slowly and, poker faced, said: 'Oh same as usual. I shall watch internet pornography for a solid twenty-four hours whilst drinking gin, pass out for a couple of days and then start again all the way through to New Year's.'

You could almost hear the thud as the secretary's lower jaw hit the desk.

'Joking, Janice,' the professor smiled, 'I shall do what I normally do and curl up with a good book – perhaps some research – in my cottage outside Hexham. I've been invited to lunch at my son's on the day but …' he shrugged.

The secretary recovered her composure and nodded. 'Have a nice time.'

Wednesday started badly.

For Rob it had begun in the early hours of the morning.

His guts had started turning over an hour after he'd eaten a curry from the take-away on his local high street, and he he'd been woken by the nagging in his stomach at about two.

By three he had installed himself in the bathroom with a bottle of water and an extra supply of toilet paper.

An hour later the stomach cramps had got worse and he had eventually thrown up and felt slightly better. 'Last time I'm using that place,' he muttered as he cold-washed his face.

By six am he had slept fitfully for only about an hour and, when he had woken, the nag had moved from his guts to his bowel. He had the distinct feeling that he was about to do something extremely childish.

On the Metro transit he had wondered if any of the other passengers could hear the symphony being played in his lower regions and walked gingerly from the station to the stage door. This start to the day was not made any better by Tom remarking that he had something of "a green tinge about the gills."

On entering the crew room he made use of the free water that was stored in bottles under the sink and sat, eyes shut, until some of the other techies turned up.

'Mornin' Rob,' greeted Harley.

Rob nodded.

Foz, Tam and Noodles were next, closely followed by Dickie.

'Feeling a bit rough, Mate?' asked Noodles.

'Dodgy curry.' was Rob's reply.

'You still eat loads of cheese?' Dickie asked as he turned on the laptop.

'Yeah. Why?'

'Y' might have tyrotoxism.'

'Tyro what?'

Dickie grinned. 'Cheese poisoning.'

'Bollocks!' Tam interjected, 'Nae such thing.'

'Oh but there is – proven fact. There's a thought-train that says...'

Rob didn't hear any more. He broke out into a horrendous sweat and made a dash for the door. Seconds later he was installed in one of the three crew toilet cubicles with the world dropping out of his backside.

THUD!

Through a haze of sweat, heat, chills and rumbling, he saw lying before him on the floor an A4 Letts diary.

'You may like to peruse that, Robert,' advised the distinctive voice of Mister Julius from the cistern above Rob's head.

'Fuck off,' he managed to gasp as his stomach cramped and un-cramped.

'Sorry, I do realise that this is not the most auspicious moment to give...'

'Julius, for fucks sake – fuck off.'

'Rob..?' came the echoing voice of Noodles from the other side of the door, 'You alright in there?'

'I'll be out in a mo',' Rob assured him.

It was more like five minutes before Rob joined the rest of the techies back in the crew room.

The greeting from Foz and Dickie, in unison, was, 'Christ!'

Noodles opted in with 'You've got food poisoning, Mate. Home.'

'I'll be okay,' Rob mumbled, 'just a bit of a bad curry.'

'Yeah! Right!.' Noodles nodded, 'Look, we can manage, and apart from that I don't want you crapping yourself on the first pull of the trap rope. Go on – get Tom to call a cab for you. See you t'morrow.'

'But…'

Fifteen minutes later and much to his relief, Rob was at home and putting the kettle on. He popped some bread in the toaster and soon he was pouring himself a large mug of hot water and with that and some dry toast he settled himself onto the settee.

The diary, with its black hard cover and gold embossing, sat on the coffee table where he had dropped it, like a bad omen.

Two slices of toast, half a cup of water, two paracetamol and a visit to the toilet later, he picked up the journal and thumbed the pages.

Before June there were various entries with regard to meetings and some cryptic scribbles, such as "ring pubshr"; "dr10"; "LitnPhil-6"; "ACLR-BACS£167". It wasn't until the mid-year date, the 16th, that Rob noticed the entry for "Panto?" and two days later another entry: "Pnto-Ring O'Leary". A fortnight later was the entry for: "1st draft – email O'L".

As the pantomime script had advanced from the first draft the entries were slightly longer and by September a scribbled margin note intrigued Rob: "Prof. Moghreb? Arabic? NUni."

Rob flicked the pages further into the year and came up to the rehearsal date that he had also attended.

The entry read. "Tiresome day. Alain obviously wants changes. Reluctant."

'You are not going to believe this,' Rob stated as he entered the crew room the following noon.

'They've cancelled the seven o'clock show and we can all go to the pub at three?' Harley asked, hopefully.

Rob shook his head. 'Sorry – not that lucky. We're here 'til ten.'

Then he withdrew the diary from inside his jacket and placed it on the seat in front of him. 'That's where the problem lies,' he stated.

'Eh?' Tam scratched his two day growth of beard, 'Y' sayin' tha' a book is why w' havin' trouble?'

Rob nodded.

'Explain?' suggested Foz.

'I haven't worked it all out yet, but some of the entries in the diary correspond with some of the stuff that's happened.'

Foz again: 'Like?'

Rob took a deep breath and picked up the book. 'Okay here we go: I quote; "break a leg seems apt for this dancer as she does not do the production justice". – same day as Zilly fell down stairs.' Rob flicked the pages of the book: '"Flys are bumping the scenery. Useless. She should be hung.".'. He flicked again, '"More flash! Yes. More flash needed for Az as he enters!"'. Rob closed the diary: 'Remind you of anything?' he asked.

There was a closed silence as the crew took in what Rob had just quoted.

'Effin twat!' Stevie eventually stated, 'Y' mean all this effin shite that we're effin putting up with is Flynn effin Forbins effin fault?'

'Couldn't have put it more succinctly myself, Stevie,' Rob answered.

Dickie pulled at a frond of his goatee: 'Okay. What do you reckon?'

Rob took a deep breath and then looked at Noodles: 'I hope you don't think that I'm undermining ...' he started.

'Rob. Fuck off. Tell us.' the reply came back.

A second breath. 'Flynn Forbins started this panto about six months ago.'

Several heads nodded in agreement.

'He then went to look for an Arabic, or whatever, phrase to supplement the Open Sez-me bit?'

Heads nodded again.

Rob sighed: 'I think that he's got some... spell...' he paused before holding up his hands in defence, '... a spell that brings beings into ... being.'

'AY!' retorted Tam, 'Th' bassard wis havin' a go at Abbynaz aboot the pronunciation o' th' "Open Sez-me" line?'

'That's right,' confirmed Harley, 'Inter-nation, or something, he said.'

'*Intonation*,' corrected Noodles.

'Has anybody got a paracetamol?' asked Noodles as he sneezed into his hands: 'Jeez! Forty quids worth!'

At that precise moment the door opened to reveal a character that was a cross between Bob Marley and Catweasle. He entered with: 'Ferk me! Aye's surprised tha' techie's axing f'asp'rin when I has pharmaceuticals tha' will send 'em through!' said the new face.

"Ian the Icy" was a regular visitor to the theatre because he supplied Front of House with ice-cream and associated products, but his mainstay was backstage where he was normally assured of sales of a different kind.

'I'z got Colombian; Afghan an' Blyth. Y'all want sometin'?'

'What the effin heck is that on your head?' asked Stevie.

'Dis my Xmas Rasta,' replied the man, pulling his multi-coloured tea-cosy hat deeper onto a black waterfall of dreadlocks.

'Well it doesn't suit you,' Harley offered.

'Oh, okay.' He removed the hat and the false hair in one move: 'Is it cos I is white?' he grinned.

'No,' replied Dickie not looking up from a book, 'it's because you have adopted a racial stereotype.'

The man looked uncomfortable for a fleeting moment and then asked in his normal voice, 'Okay anybody want any stuff?'

'You got any paracetamol?' Noodles grinned.

With a three hour break between shows the crew split off into different directions. Some went home for food, some went Christmas shopping but Rob and Noodles adjourned to the Bodger and ensconced themselves into one of the booths that lay against the left wall. They sat at opposite sides of the table and took initial sups from their beer.

'So what do you think we should do?' asked Rob, his free hand upon the diary.

'Well, we'll have to give it back at some point,' replied his drinking partner.

'Yeah, I know that. I meant about the writing.'

'You honestly believe that there is some kind of "spell"?' Noodles twitched his fingers in the air to mark the quote.

'I honestly don't see that it can be anything else. All this bother started after Forbins came on stage and said that phrase.'

'Do we know what the phrase means? It might just be some old mumbo-jumbo and a series of coincidences?'

Rob shrugged. 'I called into that kebab shop down the road, on the way in, to ask the guy in there – he's Iranian or Iraqi – but he didn't have a clue.'

'So we need to ask Forbins.' stated Noodles, reaching for his mobile phone and speed-dialling the writer's number.

After a short wait the call was answered. 'Hello, Flynn.' Noodles said in reply, 'It's Noodles from the theatre…' a muffled reply, '… yes it's about the diary. We found it in a corner of stage…'

'Phrase?' mouthed Rob.

'Yes it is intact,' Noodles nodded to Rob. 'I was wondering if you could come down to the theatre to pick it up. We're on a break between shows and in the pub next door… Bodger.'

The call ended seconds later with Noodles closing the flap on the mobile and taking a mouthful of beer.

'Well?' Rob asked.

'On his way.'

Twenty minutes later, Forbins pushed open half of the double-door entrance and, after a quick scan of the pub, made his way to the booth where Rob and Noodles sat. The diary was at the centre of the table.

The writer greeted the book with staring eyes – almost as if it were a long-lost relative – before picking it up and flicking through its pages as if the short disappearance might have caused it to lose some of its contents.

'Where did you find it?' he asked, finally.

'Under the prompt desk. Must have got kicked under there and one of the boys found it when he was sweeping up,' answered Rob by way of explanation.

'You may find that a couple of pages have picked up some dirt,' Noodles added.

While they were waiting for the writer they had opened the journal and wiped a couple of the pages across the floor of the pub by way of creating an excuse to discuss its contents.

'Couldn't help but notice that you started writing the panto in July,' said Rob as an opening gambit.

'You've read my diary?' stated the writer, affronted.

'No, no. We just wiped down some of the pages to get the fluff out.' Noodles assured him.

'There were a couple of pages that had stuck together – around about September time – but we just left those.' This had been Rob's idea – to use a small tic of chewing gum they found under the table to hold together the edges of the pages with the reference to the Arabic verse.

Forbins opened the diary and flicked the pages to the relevant entry. 'Hmm... yes...' he then carefully peeled the stuck edges of paper apart and sniffed the "glue". 'Chewing gum it would seem.'

'Important page?' Noodles prompted.

'Hmm... Oh, erm... It's just a note to myself to contact a professor at the Uni about translating a line for the play.'

'Really?' Rob feigned astonishment, 'Translating Aladdin from the "1001 Nights" so that you get authenticity?'

The author smiled. 'No, no. It was just a line that I wanted to add some… er… authenticity to the cave opening.'

Rob nodded and paused before asking, 'The one that got cut?'

'Yes' hissed Forbins.

'Happens in all the best productions, though, doesn't it?'

'Hnn… Let me buy you gentlemen a drink. It's the least I can do for returning this.' He slipped the diary into the satchel-style briefcase that was slung from his shoulder. 'What will you have?'

While the writer queued at the bar Noodles and Rob held a whispered conversation that had just ended when the drinks were placed on the table.

'I hope you don't mind if I join you?' Forbins asked, sliding next to Noodles with a large glass of red wine.

'Not at all.' he replied, moving along the bench seat and silently breathing a sigh of relief.

'Panto seems to be going well?' Rob opened.

'Yes. Well.' Forbins replied ambivalently.

'You don't sound too… well… enthused, if I may put it that way?'

Forbins cradled the wine glass in both hands and ran his thumbs across the rim as if using it as a shriving bowl. 'It's only the second time that I've written this sort of thing. The first was for a company in the south of England. It was very well received,' he explained, adding pensively, 'not as many cuts or problems.'

'And you added authenticity to that one as well?'

'Little bit of Welsh. Seemed to go down well with the locals,' he nodded.

'So a bit of Arabic in this…' started Noodles.

'Oh it's not Arabic. It's a precursor to that language. A professor at the Uni had discovered an old series of tracts written in the Moghreb language.' Forbins took a sip of his wine. 'It's sort of bygone Persian.

I heard about it in a local newspaper and thought that it sounded just the thing for this.'

Rob and Noodles exchanged the briefest of glances.

'Shit!' exclaimed Rob, slapping his forehead. 'You know what we didn't ask him?'

They had just entered the stage door to return for the second show.

'What?'

'Noodles, what the hell do the words mean?'

'Ah! … ring the professor to find out?' the tech manager suggested.

As Noodles signed the attendance sheet, Rob leafed through the phone book that dangled by a cord next to the stage door pay-phone kiosk.

He dialled the number and waited impatiently for an answer.

'Ladies and gentlemen, this is your half hour call,' stated the voice from the Tannoy.

'Hello. University. Sharon speaking. How may I help you?'

'I'm trying to contact a professor who's involved in translating old Persian,' Rob stated.

'One moment.' Three or four bars of tinny music assaulted Rob as the telephonist put him on hold. The line clicked back in. 'That would be Professor Vauxhall. He's left for the holidays, but I can take a message for when he returns in the New Year.'

'Oh, I see. Is there any way of contacting him before then?'

'One moment.'

More tinny music and then the line clicked again.

'Professor Vauxhall's secretary. How may I help?'

'Yes… er… Flynn Forbins here, writer,' Rob lied, trying to emulate the writer's speech. 'The professor was doing some translation for me and I was hoping to receive it before Christmas. I understand he's left

for the holidays but I'm afraid I have a deadline. He did promise…'
Rob trailed off.

'The professor has left for the holidays and is out of contact at
present. The cottage doesn't have a phone and his mobile doesn't
work unless he goes into Hexham proper.'

'Oh, I see. Well thank you any way I…' and at that point Rob
pressed the receiver down button.

'No joy, I take it?' asked Noodles.

'Not there. Gone for his Xmas break. But…' Rob grinned.

'But?'

'He's up by Hexham… somewhere.'

'Why don't we just ask Forbins?'

'I doubt he's in any state to ask at present. He was well into his
fourth glass when we left.'

Noodles slowly nodded by way of agreement.

'So what are you looking for?' Dickie asked.

'Googling – for a Professor in a cottage,' Rob replied, having
taken the crew room laptop to the Bodger, to take advantage of the
free wi-fi.

'I met a vicar in a cottage once,' offered Tom, with a sly look and
then smiling as sweetly as if butter wouldn't melt in his mouth.

'Not THAT kind of cottage! This one's up by Hexham.'

'Hmm…' Tom threw back at him, 'mine was down the
Quayside.'

'Any joy?' Noodles asked.

'Nah! Found out that he lives in Hexham but as for the cottage…
nada.'

'M'be a neighbour wid know?' Tam suggested, taking interest and
looking up from his pint.

Rob nodded.

Noodles suggested: 'If anyone's got a car we could have a trip out on Monday? Day off.'

'No tax, no MOT, a bit clapped out but it'll get there,' Dickie held up a finger to offer his services.

Grins spread around the table.

They met in the Bodger at opening time and five minutes later Dickie's car had pulled up. A rusting Mercedes that was, or had been, an orange cum gold colour.

'Anyone for the skylark?' asked the driver, popping his head around the door.

Rob and Noodles gulped down the last of their beer and were soon ensconced in the rear seat of the vehicle.

'It might be old, but it goes fast,' Dickie promised.

'Bit like you, then?' Rob answered.

Pulling away from the kerb it was not long before they were on the A69 towards Hexham and from the congested roundabout that *ought* to have been a slip road they turned off into the Northumbrian town. Not long after crossing the bridge and circumnavigating a roundabout they pulled left into the town's car park.

Above them was the steep slope up to the abbey, the old gaol and the market square.

'Battle plan?' asked Dickie after getting a parking permit from the vending machine and sticking it to the inside of the windscreen.

'If he's in a cottage then I reckon he owns it,' Noodles stated, 'so who to ask about it?'

'Estate agents?' Dickie suggested.

'Nah! It's not for sale,' Rob stated.

'Could be he gets into the abbey?' Noodles shrugged.

'Good a place as any to start,' Dickie answered.

They left the car park and wound their way up the steep hill towards the market square and the beautiful church, entering by the side doorway – their footsteps echoed slightly as they trooped down the aisle.

'Good morning... sorry, afternoon.' said a person that seemed to have suddenly appeared at Rob's shoulder, 'would you care for the tour?'

The middle aged, bearded and bespectacled man was clutching a ream of pamphlets to the breast of his finely chequered suit.

'Er... no thanks,' answered Rob, somewhat disconcerted, 'we're looking for someone.'

The guide's friendly demeanour dropped several points.

'That is er...' Rob continued, 'someone who may attend the abbey.'

'Oh! I do know several of our regular visitors and worshippers. Who is it you are looking for?'

'Professor Vauxhall.' Rob replied, then offered, 'Professor James Vauxhall, he's at the University in Newcastle?'

The man clutched his pamphlets even tighter and shook his head: 'No. No. Can't say I recognise the name.'

'Okay, thanks.'

Just as the tour guide was about to turn and walk away he stopped: 'Have you tried the bookshop?'

'Bookshop?'

'Yes. The one down St Mary's Chare, Cog... Cog-something. If he's a professor he's bound to have called in there. Great range of books and compact discs.' smiled the guide.

'Thanks.' said Noodles.

'Yeah, thanks,' repeated Rob, 'We'll give it a try.'

The double-fronted, green painted, shop was indeed just around the corner and as the three men entered a small bell rattled above the door.

'Good afternoon. Can I help?' said a voice from somewhere behind a bookcase.

'Er…' Dickie started.

The bookseller appeared around a set of shelves. A stocky man of well over six feet with a military bearing approached them with a smile that bristled his moustache.

'Just looking.' stated Noodles.

'Anything particular?' asked the man sticking his thumbs into his red braces.

'Thought you might have something by Professor James Vauxhall

- him being local,' replied Rob, taking the initiative.

'Ah, James… no. All his stuff is published by the university. He's a bit too academic for around here.'

'But he does live locally?' Dickie jumped in.

'Yes. Very nice place up the bank, beside the river.'

'And he has a cottage… locally I understand?' Rob thought he would jump in with both feet.

'Up at Wark. Nice place. One of those "roses-around-the-door" places,' the bookseller agreed with a smile, 'probably why it's called "Rose Forge Cottage".'

Excusing themselves from the shop and making their way back down the bank to the car park, they were soon pouring over a map of the local area.

'Wark,' stated Dickie, 'Pronounced "Waark". Out of Hexham, left, on a bit, turn right onto the 6079, carry on, turn left, carry on – can't miss it'

'Looks like the whole place would fit into the theatre,' observed Noodles.

Twenty minutes later they pulled up into the rear car park of the Battlesteads Hotel, Wark's busy village hostelry.

'Why've you pulled in here, Dickie?' Rob asked.

'Local intelligentsia and I are bloody hungry,' he retorted.

They followed the entrance directions through a small corridor to the front of the building that was decorated with ersatz wooden beams and lime-washed walls. The empty bar was to their right, with a dining area beyond, and a roaring fire to their left. They headed to the bar where a tall, skinny man was lounging. His nameplate announced him as "Mike".

'Afternoon gentlemen!' he greeted, 'What can I get you?'

After ordering two Guinness and a cola for Dickie they were invited to take a seat by the fire – the barman would bring over the order of the local Belsay beef sandwiches.

They made themselves comfortable on a three-seater sofa and a voluminous armchair.

'Nice place,' stated Noodles.

'Not bad prices either,' noted Rob, flicking through a flyer for the hotel.

They made small talk until their sandwiches were delivered by Mike.

'Not very busy?' asked Noodles, as he put their plates, napkins and cutlery on the table in front of them, together with a rack of condiments.

'No, not very. This is the run-up. Christmas. Come tomorrow we'll be stowed off with diners and lunchtime will be panicsville.'

'Suppose you know everyone around here?' asked Rob flattening the overstuffed sandwich and squirting gravy onto his jeans.

'Just about,' he agreed.

'Farmers… Doctors… Professors?' Rob suggested, tentatively.

'Oh aye. One lives over the road.' He nodded his head to the right. 'Stays up here every Christmas. Works at the Uni in Newcastle. Professor… er… car… Vauxhall.'

'Really?' Rob enquired.

'He'll be in shortly. Large brandy and a packet of pork scratchings,' the barman replied from memory.

Three satisfied smiles passed around the table and devoured their sandwiches.

They had hardly finished dusting down the seeds from the bread and wiping their mouths when the ante-door squeaked open and a short man in tweeds and Wellington boots entered. As he removed his brown trilby he nodded to the stage crew before approaching the bar.

'A'noon, Prof.' stated Mike, 'usual?'

'Yes please Michael, and one for yourself.'

'Very kind, I'll take a half of Magus, if I may.'

The learned man nodded and passed across a twenty pound note with, 'I believe I had a tab last evening. That should cover it.'

While the barman calculated the professor's debt he made his way to the cheerful blaze in the fireplace and warmed his rump.

'Chilly isn't it?' opened Vauxhall. 'Come for a run out?'

'Yeah,' replied Noodles, 'Dickie thought a spot of fresh air might do us good after being in the theatre all week.' He nodded towards their driver.

'Ah! Theatre? Which one?'

'Herald Royal,' replied Rob, 'in Newcastle.'

'Yes, yes. I know it. In fact if you are the chaps that are doing Aladdin I had a small part to play in it – if you'll pardon the pun?'

'Really?' replied Rob, smiling disingenuously.

'Yes. The writer chap wanted me to do a translation for him. Something about stones…'

'"Under my command and move when I say so" – or something to that effect?' probed Noodles.

'Yes, yes. Something like that.' He flipped a handkerchief to his nose and gave a brief sneeze followed by a knowing smile. 'More medicine, I think.' He fetched a refill from the bar, and his change.

'You were saying … ?' asked Rob.

'Sorry. Yes. Vauxhall. James Vauxhall. I'm a professor at the Uni in Newcastle. Ancient languages… that sort of thing.'

'Ah, you'll know Flynn Forbins?' offered Dickie.

The professor's demeanour changed slightly. 'Yes. Bit of a pest really. I said I'd do his translation but completely forgot about it,' he grimaced, 'left it 'til the last minute. Gave him a bit of guff really.'

'Oh?' probed Rob.

'I was in the middle of a translation of an old Moghreb document when he rang, and I'd been working since about six that morning, I carelessly gave him the word for "statue" instead of "stone". Silly really, not that it matters for this purpose, eh?' he threw back the brandy and popped open his packet of pork rinds.

'This Moghreb document?' Rob enquired, 'Old is it?'

The professor chuckled, 'So old as to carry a health warning.'

'Oh?'

'Some chaps at Harvard discovered it and it came with a codicil that warned against chanting any of the words out loud'. He laughed again and proceeded to get yet another brandy from the bar.

'Okay, okay!' Noodles held up his hands in the car park. 'Sorry for doubting you.'

'A friggin' warning on a bit of old writing...' Dickie shook his head as he opened the doors to the car.

'Makes you think, though.' Rob grinned.

As the trio headed back down the road towards Newcastle they discussed the events of the day and when Dickie pulled up outside Rob's house he invited them in. 'Cigars and Brandy, Mates, courtesy of HM Customs? Dickie – there's a spare bed for a 'tired' driver?'

Within a few moments snifters were poured, and Rob had passed around the bright yellow box of "Elegantes". They snipped the ends off with loving care.

'I reckon... ' Rob exhaled a long stream of fragrant smoke into the air of the living room '...that we need to keep the writer out of the theatre so as to keep the production on a level peg?'

'Totally agreed,' stated Noodles, raising his glass of "103".

'Anything the writer writes goes into the ether and the dirty angel acts on it. So, yes, agreed.' Dickie took a sip of the amber liquid.

'Problem is, how do we get the old bugger to stay away?'

The ashtray held numerous cigar butts, the room smelt of the smoke residue and the bottle of brandy was lying empty.

Noodles had passed out in the armchair and was snoring.

No sign of Dickie as Rob risked opening an eye from his overnight on the settee. He glanced at the mantle clock – twenty past ten – time for a cuppa.

As Rob rattled around in the kitchen he heard stirrings from the room above – he presumed it was Dickie – and Noodles awoke with a start and the greeting of: 'Bugger!'

'Tea?' Rob shouted.

A muffled "Yeah" from above and an "ung-huh" from the living room encouraged him to drop three tea-bags into mugs, followed by steaming water, milk and sugar. He carried the brews into the living room just as Dickie entered.

'Mornin" the man grinned as he fastened the top button on his black jeans and then proceeded to tuck in his tee-shirt, 'You two must be getting old.'

Noodles looked at him, red eyed: 'Huh? I'm ten, twenty years... thingy.'

Dickie chortled. 'You two passed out and I spent the night under a rather warm duck-down duvet.'

Rob remembered buying that for his mother one winter. 'Comfy night, eh?'

Dickie smiled. 'Hope you didn't mind but I just hit the first room I came to.'

Rob shook his head and made to sip his tea.

'Why do I feel like a rangy-arsed badger's been asleep in my mouth?' asked Noodles of no-one in particular.

Both Dickie and Rob exchanged glances and looked smug.

'Lack of practice?' offered Rob as he took another sip of the sweet tea.

'Time 'sit?'

'Nearly half ten,' was the reply.

'Bollocks!' repeated the tech manager, 'We've got to be in for twelve. Pay call.'

Dickie drove, via a roadside van that did a line in hot sandwiches and something called a "Geordie Kebab" – half a stottie loaf packed with sausage, bacon, egg, mushrooms, black pudding and beans – to the theatre, and parked up in the free bay opposite the stage door.

'How's your head, Mate?' Rob asked Noodles.

'Better for the breakfast,' was the reply as he attempted to wipe some bean sauce from his tee-shirt.

'Pay call in fifteen minutes in the Green Room,' announced a male voice over the Tannoy as they entered the stage door.

'T.F.I.F.' Tam spelt out, joining them as they walked into the stage entrance, 'Basta'd o' a night at th' casino.'

They ensconced themselves in the crew room and once they were all assembled, Rob delivered the startling information that they had found out on their trip into the Northumbrian countryside.

'So it *is* an effin spell' from Stevie.

'Too bleeding right,' from Dickie.

'Professors can't be wrong,' from Noodles.

'Guid job we've a dirty angel up theer.' from Tam, pointing a finger towards the roof.

'Eh?' asked Rob, 'How's that?'

Tam chuckled: 'A few yards doon th' road y've a naked bird atop a clock,' he referred to the insignia of a goldsmith's store at the junction further down the street from the theatre.

'But she's not Persian.' Harley responded.

'Ach, no, she's no'. *Perishin'* aye,' the Scot grinned.

'Pay call, five minutes,' blurted the Tannoy.

'When I came past the other day she was wearing a football jersey,' Dickie remarked.

'Students.' Tam nodded, 'Time was when sh's on a rag week sh'd be wearin' bra and knickers. This year it was a thong.'

'What!' Harley interjected with an irate voice, 'No bra?'

'Sign of the times,' nodded Noodles, still feeling slightly hung over.

'Pay call time,' stated Rob nodding at the clock, so they trooped across stage to the green room. The door was firmly shut.

'Gimmee th' money!' pleaded Tam.

'Paaaaaay!' chided Harley.

Paul Bigg came from the dressing room 1 corridor to the entrance to the green room and looked suspiciously at the door: 'Er… what's going on? Is Amble not here?' he asked referring to the accountant that had paid them every week so far with a flurry of white envelopes and the flourish of a pen to sign for that which was gratefully received.

'Nope!' the chorus came from those cast and crew assembled.

He rattled the door and then used the flat of his hand to pound upon it. 'Amble?'

The accountant appeared from the crew toilet at the end of the corridor: 'Sorry, guys. Caught short,' he blustered, 'pay call as of now.' he let himself into the room with a key.

A general "Hurrah" went up amongst those waiting.

'Er…' The accountant stood in the doorway as if dumbstruck.

'Er, what?' asked Paul Biggs.

'Er, like … where's the cashbox?' was the reply.

'Cashbox?' asked Bigg.

As the accountant entered the room the lights dimmed slightly and then flickered back.

Two envelopes were in the middle of the floor. One read "Rob Crowther" the other "Noodles Sawyer" and banknotes were spilling from them. The cashbox that held the other wage packets was gone.

No-one had been paid and the two envelopes had been retained by Amber – they hadn't called the police in to investigate as Noodles had reassured Biggs, Liddle and O'Leary that the money would be found by the end of the show.

'Ladies and gentlemen, this is your beginners' call. Gentlemen of the orchestra to the pit and beginners to stage please. Crew to positions.' rang the Tannoy with Sam's voice.

The show was slow and slightly half-hearted.

In the prompt side wing Rob had stated, 'I'm going to see someone,' just before the interval. 'This crap has got to stop!' and he left by the off-stage door.

'Where's he gone?' asked Harley.

'Crap,' Dickie stated.

Rob locked the door of the cubicle, lowered the lid of the toilet seat and sat down. He waited.

Eventually he said: 'Julius if you're there, just answer.'

No reply.

'Julius?' Rob hissed.

Still no answer.

'Julius you had better get back to me here 'cause if you don't the next person in this cubicle will be wearing a dog collar, speaking Latin and sprinkling water. Heads will spin!'

'I'm not supposed to.' Julius's voice, echoing slightly, came from above Rob's head milliseconds later.

'I don't give a monkey's tadger whether you're supposed to or not. Where's the money?'

'Money? What money?'

'Don't you give me any of your perfidious bullshit. You lot know everything that goes on in here.'

There was silence for a moment and Rob could hear the end of the first act come down to the door-muffled applause of the audience.

'Julius!' he hissed again.

'I would look in the cistern over the urinal,' stated the echoing voice.

Rob dashed from the lavatory and onto the stage where he beckoned to Noodles, who was standing beside the prompt desk waiting for the safety curtain to be brought in to the stage.

While the steel fire barrier was being lowered he ran into the dock area and grabbed a set of A-frame step ladders and met Noodles, together with Dan O'Leary, in costume, next to the off stage door.

'I've an idea where the wages are,' Rob stated, pulling open the door. 'Humour me will you?' he said to O'Leary.

Making their way to the end of the corridor he erected the ladder beneath the gurgling cistern that was close to the ceiling and, after handing down the lid to Noodles, rolled up his sleeve and plunged his hand into the freezing water. He felt about the bottom of the tank and with a whispered 'eureka' withdrew the buff box that held the wages.

'How the..?' started O'Leary.

'Hunch' was Rob's laconic reply. 'We need to have a meeting. Urgently.'

The actor nodded.

After the show had finished, and everyone had been paid – thanks in part to the wardrobe department having ironed out a few of the problems with wet banknotes – Bigg, Liddle, O'Leary, Noodles and Rob were the only ones in the Green Room.

O'Leary closed the door and slipped the latch so that no one could enter. Turning to face those assembled he stared straight at Rob. 'You've something to tell us about the cash going missing?'

'You're not going to believe what I'm going to tell you, but yes.'

'When did you take it?'

'What!'

'When did you take it?' the actor repeated.

'Hang on a minute...' interjected Noodles, 'Rob found the money. Are you trying to imply that he nicked it?'

'How else would he know where it had been hidden? I'm afraid that I don't believe in a "hunch".'

Rob took a deep breath: 'As I started to say, you are not going to believe what I'm going to tell you.'

Half an hour later Rob, with some help from Noodles, had related that the incidents that had happened were all down to the writer; their trip to Wark; how the speaking of the Persian phrase had somehow influenced events and the writing that had appeared on the lift mirror that had led them to the roof.

O'Leary and the other two producers listened carefully and nodded as Rob related the tale – but they had not interrupted.

'That still doesn't tell us how you knew where the money was?' Bigg stated when Rob had finished.

'The same way that I found the diary.' Rob replied.

'A ghost?' demanded Liddle incredulously.

Rob sighed. 'Believe it or not, I couldn't have nicked the money. Amble was in here with the box; he went for a piss; came back to a locked room and all the time I was in the crew room with the rest of the lads.'

'A ghost?' repeated Liddle.

'I said you wouldn't believe me. The problem we have is to keep Flynn Forbins out of the theatre. Whatever he writes in his diary... it happens.'

'He was in this morning.' Bigg noted, 'getting his final payment for the script from Amber.'

'Bingo!' exclaimed Noodles, 'and I'd like to bet a pound to a pinch of shit that he made a jotting in his journal?'

Rob pulled his mobile phone from the back pocket of his jeans and flicked the phonebook to find the writer's number. He pressed *dial* and passed the handset to O'Leary. 'Go on. Ask him.'

O'Leary stared at the phone for a moment, accepted it from Rob, but then flipped it shut cutting the connection. 'Okay… If you're that sure?'

Rob nodded: 'We are *that* sure.'

'This Mugreb… Magrub phrase…' started Liddle.

'Moghreb' Noodles corrected.

'Moghreb phrase' Liddle continued, 'how do we know what it means and how is it doing what it's doing? I mean, a centuries' old piece of writing suddenly brings to life a statue in the theatre? You have to admit it's a bit far fetched.'

'I would have applied that old theatre axiom of "shit happens" if I didn't know any better,' Rob replied, 'but I do.'

'I'm with Rob,' Noodles concurred.

After the second show the Tannoy called Rob and Noodles to dressing room one.

'M'be it's a bonus f' finding th' wedge?' Tam grinned as he riffled the notes in his open wallet.

Rob knocked at the door.

'Yeah! Come in.' O'Leary was in his civvies and was combing his hair in front of a mirror surrounded by forty watt bulbs.

'Dan?' asked Noodles.

'We're going for a run out. Overnighter, but we'll be back for the show tomorrow.' He put the comb down on the bench next to his array of makeup. 'If you haven't got a toothbrush then the hotel will find one, I'm sure.'

'Er… where are we going?' Rob asked.

'To get to the bottom of this. A professor in Wark.'

They were met at the stage door by a people-carrier driven by Bigg. Liddle sat in the rear, and he moved across the seat to allow Rob and

Noodles to sit together. O'Leary jumped in the front. Within ten minutes they were speeding westwards towards the Northumbrian countryside.

It transpired that during the breaks from the show O'Leary had made several telephone calls. He had booked rooms for them at the hotel and arranged a breakfast conference with Professor Vauxhall. He had also spoken to Flynn Forbins and had eventually prised out of him that he had indeed made an entry in his diary – to the effect that that he should have been paid more, or at least have had a return on the gate receipts.

Within fifty-five minutes, Bigg was turning the vehicle off the road and around to the back of the hotel to park up.

'I'll go and book us in,' stated O'Leary opening the passenger door. 'I'll see you lot in the bar.'

Ten minutes later saw the comedy duo and the two techies, having ordered beers from Mike, again sitting next to the fireplace in a half full bar. It seemed to be populated mainly with locals – many dressed in Wellingtons and Barbour jackets.

O'Leary walked into the bar with a handful of keys and a short, red-haired, woman on his arm who, from her posture, Rob assumed had been a dancer.

'Rob, Noodles, this is Chrissie, my wife. Thought I might make an outing of it.'

The woman smiled at the two and nodded but said nothing.

O'Leary held out the keys with their heavy brass fobs and then threw one set at the comics and another at Rob and Noodles. 'Sorry Boys, but you got the short straw. Paul and Michael a twin; me and Chrissie a double. You're sleeping together. Sorry, it's a double, last room in the house,' he explained. 'But you do have a Jacuzzi.'

'Oh, we'll be the talk of the stage door tomorrow,' lisped Noodles, and then minced towards the bar, the key dangling from a limp wrist.

Mike approached the table with a cloth over his arm in true waiter fashion: 'Your meals are ready Mister O'Leary. If you wouldn't mind?' he proffered a hand towards the dining area at the far end of the bar.

'Thanks. Yeah, great. It's good of your boss to sort us at such short notice. I've left some comp tickets at reception.'

Noodles and Rob exchanged glances. 'Food?' mouthed Rob.

Noodles shrugged.

As they took their seats at a table set for six, a young girl in a white apron and a black dress opened a bottle of red wine and then placed an ice bucket with a bottle of white on the table. Within moments they had each been served a plate of steak with all the trimmings.

'Just like being on tour,' thought Rob as he shovelled meat and potatoes into his mouth.

After their meal the company adjourned to their seats beside the fire. The crowd had thinned out to two young couples, obviously residents as their keys lay before them on the bar.

Bigg ordered more wine and they settled down for what was clearly going to be a conference.

O'Leary opened with, 'As we've got a two o'clock show tomorrow I've arranged a ten am meeting with this professor. Now, Rob, Noodles, tell me everything you know about this Moghreb phenomenon.'

Rob spent a restless night. For one, the bedroom was too hot for his taste and the other problem was that Noodles snored like a buzz-saw on overdrive. By six am he had retired to the en-suite bathroom and had lowered himself into the bubbling Jacuzzi.

An hour later he was towelling himself dry when there was a knock on the door.

'Rob?'

'Yeah. Come in.' he wrapped the towel around himself and pushed his fingers through his hair.

Noodles came through the doorway wearing candy stripe boxer shorts. 'Wondered where you'd got to. Must take a piss.'

Rob left Noodles to his ablutions and returned to the bedroom to get dressed.

By nine o'clock Rob had stood outside the hotel entrance and smoked a couple of cigarettes – before indulging in three large cups of tea in the bar area. He was feeling almost human again and was about to light up a third cigarette, in the courtyard, when he saw the professor, with a satchel over his shoulder, approaching the hostelry across the fine frost that glinted on the grass verge in the morning sun.

'Good morning,' he greeted, 'it's... Rob isn't it?'

'Morning, Professor. Yeah. Here for the meeting?'

'Indeed. Most curious, according to Mister O'Leary. Seems I may have stirred up a hornets' nest.'

'Something like that,' replied Rob flicking his unfinished smoke towards a large plant pot, half full of sand.

'I'm slightly early, I think,' the academic shrugged, 'so time for a coffee.'

By ten thirty Rob had again repeated what had happened in the theatre and had explained that he and Noodles believed that the Moghreb phrase was responsible.

Throughout, the professor listened to the story with his fingers pinched together under his chin, nodding sagely now and again.

All heads then turned to the learned man.

'Well, what do you think, Professor?' asked O'Leary.

'To use the vernacular; "well I never did",' the man guffawed.

'So it's plausible?' asked Liddle.

'Perfectly. The tracts that I'm studying were found in the north eastern part of Iraq, just after the war started, by a former history student that happened to be part of the American armed forces. He sent them state-side and they've been pored over ever since by academics throughout the world. We're trying to make sense of them as they appear to be unrelated phrases.'

'In my position as genie of the lamp,' smiled Bigg, putting down his coffee cup, 'I would suggest that it's a list of incantation spells.'

Liddle nodded: 'What's happened is we've put two and two together and come up with four – by accident.'

Vauxhall held up a finger: 'These statues were … requisitioned shall we say … from a Persian temple before being installed at the theatre. Does anyone know the actual provenance of them?'

'Only thing I could find was that they were taken from Persia by Sir Jeffery Armstrong.' Rob stated, 'Found that out on the web.'

'Hmm… in that case…' the professor reached into to his satchel and took from it a laptop; he opened the lid and started it up. ' We shall also take advantage of the web and use the free wi-fi that is available in here.'

By noon the professor had trawled through academic sites – not available to the general public – and every site, including the spurious ones, on the internet. Finally he sat back and picked up his sheaf of notes, closing his computer with a firm click. 'Babylon,' he stated.

'Babylon?' chorused Bigg and Liddle.

'Babylon, the legendary city, indeed, the most famous ancient city in the whole world,' stated the academic. 'It was the capital of ten Mesopotamian dynasties starting with King Hammurabi, the sixth king of the first dynasty, reaching prominence as the capital city of the great kingdom of Babylonia. The last dynasty, during which Babylon achieved its zenith, is well known particularly for its second king, Nebuchadnezzar.' He smiled.

'An eight-foot stele, pillaged from Babylon by an Elamite King – found in 1901 by French archaeologists in Susa the ancient Elamite capital – has Babylonian cuneiform writing. This writing is three thousand lines of "The Code" – King Hammurabi's lasting monument. A sort of common law.

'To the east of the Babylonian Street of Processions lies Nin Makh's Temple – I believe that this is where the statues were plundered from as it is also where we have researched the Moghreb language, not only from the Code but also from other writings found there.'

'So how does this help us?' O'Leary asked.

'To be perfectly frank – it doesn't. However, we can now assume a slight provenance on the statues, knowing where they came from. I shall have to email colleagues to find more.'

'So we're still up shit creek with no bog brush?' Liddle stated.

The professor shrugged: 'Until I can get confirmation from other academics I would suggest that you keep this chap, Forbins, out of the theatre.'

'Your lad still doing computery things?' Rob asked Stevie.

'Effin right! Lucky sod just scored for a effin 35k job with some effin software company.'

They were in the crew room just before the half, drinking tea.

'So it'd be no problem for him to set up a vid-cam on the roof and link it to a web page that we could monitor?' Noodles enquired.

Stevie shrugged. 'Nah! No effin prob. He could do that in his effin sleep. Wouldn't even need to set up a effin web page. Straight effin through.'

'... yes that's what I said. Persona non grata. Just 'til we sort out this problem with front of house...' O'Leary sighed as the writer ranted. '... yes I fully understand but it's better that you don't come in at the moment.'

The call lasted another four or five minutes.

'Yes. Just 'til we get sorted out. I'll ring you... 'bye.'

The Christmas Eve show had passed without incident, and Rob had walked the few yards from the stage door round the corner to The Bodger only to find that it was closed. He made his way back to the theatre.

'Bodger shut?' asked Tom.

'Yup.'

Tom nodded, 'Same as last year. Only places open'll be the Star, down the street or the gay.'

'The gay?'

'"Woofy Pup". I'm going. Lots of "friends".' he grinned.

The switchboard phone rang and Tom answered it, slightly frustrated. He had his coat on and was ready for his "friends".

'Yes, still here,' he held out the phone to Rob, 'one of your girlfriends...' he mouthed, salaciously.

'Hello?'

'Can you get me in tonight, Robert?'

'Lil?'

'Tonight?'

'Er... er...' stumbling his words he wracked his brain to try and explain, in the nicest possible way, why he couldn't let the old lady into the theatre – apart from the fact that there would be no-one there and it was shut.

'It's got to be tonight Robert,' she pleaded, 'it's got to be.'

'But Lil, you're still in hospital...'

'Bollocks... tonight... please?'

It was, Rob thought, probably the only chance he would have to let Lil into the theatre before...

From his visits between shows it seemed to him that she wanted to see the show rather than that she needed to see the theatre.

'Yeah. Okay. I'll see what I can do.'

'You must promise...'

'Okay.'

The trip to the gay bar with Tom had borne fruit. After several large pink gins the stage door keeper had divulged, with some careful prompting on Robs behalf, that the locks on the theatre doors had only half been changed when the new company had taken over. Front of house had been replaced, as had the stage door, but the others had not.

'So the old dock fire escape...' asked Rob referring to the small door that nuzzled the edge of the scene dock and was a mere pass door when the dock was crowded.

'Open to the world, love.' Tom had slurred. 'Burglar alarms don't work – bastards wouldn't spend the money – so anyone could steal the theatre.'

Rob made his excuses, after a further half an hour, and called a cab.

'I understand that the device that Mister Crowther has installed on the roof is working correctly. That and they are keeping the writer out of the place?'

'Yes Mama.'

'Things are going to come to a head very shortly Bertie, you do know this?'

'Yes Mama.'

'We shall have to help Mister Crowther, and the rest of the stage crew, to rectify this position or we are going to be...' Her Ladyship searched for the correct phrase.

'Lumbered, Mama?'

'Aptly put Bertie. We shall be lumbered with this... thing – forever. I am revoking the talk rules as from now – even though Julius has been slightly naughty and spoken to Mister Crowther'

Lil was sat up in bed with the covers pulled up to her chin – all the pipes and wires had now been removed.

'You are going to get me into trouble,' remonstrated Rob. 'Why tonight?'

'You'll see,' she stated throwing back the bed clothes, to reveal that she was fully dressed, and gingerly stepping out of the bed.

Rob pushed the wheelchair, which had been conveniently left in the dayroom, towards the edge of the bed, and she flopped into it.

'I hate being old,' Lil stated.

'You're still fit, Lil.'

'Hah! You just get me to the theatre.'

'Sorry I'm late. I had to go and get my old keys.' Rob's taxi journey had taken him to the terraced house and to the trunk where his theatre gear had been stored. In a corner was the spare bunch of keys that he had used in his capacity as stage manager. One of those keys would let him into the premises.

'Get my medicine and that brown leather folded picture-frame from my bedside cabinet before we go, please' the old lady instructed.

Rob dropped the side of the unit open and found the picture frame immediately.

'I don't see any medication, Lil'

'Bottom cupboard.'

'Lucozade and that bottle of "103" I got you?'

'That's it.'

'Brandy!... You're…'

'Yes I'm sure. Now come on before those nice girls do their rounds and find me like this.'

The corridors were empty as Rob pushed Lil's wheelchair towards the lift. He pressed the button for the basement car park and eventually emerged beside the waiting cab.

When he finally got Lil into her seat he noticed that the meter read over twenty pounds.

'Herald Royal Theatre' he instructed the driver, 'drop us at the stage door.'

'I do believe we are about to have guests' stated Her Ladyship.
'Guests Mama?'
'Indeed, Bertie. The sibling of one of our own is to visit. Please inform Doris that she is required to meet her sister in the Upper Circle in a very short time.. and Bertie?'
'Yes Mama?'
'She is to take a certain something with her.'

The cab's final bill was nearly thirty pounds. Rob passed across two twenties as the driver dropped the wheelchair loading platform to street level.

It was sleeting slightly as Rob pushed the unwieldy chair down past the stage door, up the side street and into the back lane where the dark loading dock was located.

Rob took from his belt his small Maglite torch, turned it on and placed it between his teeth; he then searched through the bunch of keys that he had taken from his pocket until he recognised one of them. It was only seconds before he was bumping Lil and the wheelchair up a series of stone stairs towards the stage.

From there, he used the pass door to access the theatre proper and used the lift to get to the Upper Circle.

He was out of breath as he pushed open the spring-loaded door to the semi-circular seating, illuminated by the emergency lights.

'Upper circle' he rasped, still out of breath.

'Row C, fourth one in,' instructed Lil.

'Do you mind if I lift you down there? It's just going to be a... a pain to bump the chair.'

'Not at all, Robert. Haven't had a man lift me anywhere for years.' she grinned.

'Lil,' Rob stated, 'you're insatiable.'

Rob lifted the old lady in his arms – she must have weighed all of six stone, if that – and carried her to the third row from the front of the barrier that surrounded the public area.

'Fourth one in? Left or right?' Rob asked.

'Left,' was Lil's reply, 'and then get out the brandy.'

Rob pushed the flap-up seat down with his foot and gently placed her onto it. He then sat down next to her and reached into his blouson for the picture frame and the bottle. He passed them to Lil.

'That's our Doris,' Lil stated, opening the frame and showing Rob a black and white picture of a good looking girl in a floral dress and sporting a beehive hair-do. 'She got murdered right here.'

Rob nodded, unsure of what to say.

'She's a ghost now.' Lil stated, unscrewing the top from the "103" and taking a healthy swig. 'Merry Christmas, Mister Crowther.' She passed the bottle to Rob.

'Merry Christmas, Lil.' Rob drank deeply from the bottle and then wiped his hand across his mouth.

They sat in silence for a few minutes, sipping the liquor, before Lil asked: 'What time is it?'

Rob drew his pocket watch from his jeans, after glancing first at the Canarian watch to find it said six o'clock, and popped open the lid: 'Just coming up to midnight,' he stated.

'Would you mind moving across the aisle? I need to talk to someone.'

Rob had barely taken his seat when a blue swirl moved over the balcony and then turned into a globe of light that hovered over the seat next to Lil. Once in position it transformed into a shadow of the photograph that Lil had shown him.

Rob sat transfixed as the ghost sister and the old lady held a hushed conversation. Realising that he still held the bottle of brandy

Rob took a deep mouthful; he blinked several times and caught his breath.

The shadow vanished as quickly as it had appeared, turning back into a blue light and then zooming across the auditorium and through the safety curtain to disappear.

'Thank you, Rob,' whispered Lil, looking across from her seat. 'Would you take me back to the hospital please?'

Rob was still feeling upset when he finally opened his front door. He'd had an argument with the night nurse about the Lil's absence – he'd offered the explanation that she'd 'been in the toilet', but understandably it hadn't rung true.

'Not for *two hours*, Mister Crowther! Our nurses check every half hour. Where have you been with her?'

He had eventually told her, in no uncertain terms, to 'Fuck right off!'

As he lit a much needed cigar his phone rang.

'Hello?'

'Mister Crowther?'

'Yes?'

'Could you come to the hospital, please? I'm afraid that it's your mother.'

Having said his last goodbye to Lil, as she lay still and grey in the hospital bed, he had to explain to the doctor that he wasn't really her son and that Barry was.

After several frustrating phone calls he tried to convince the hospital gauleiters that because of adverse weather conditions in the North Sea, in the short term he would have to sort out anything to do with Lil.

'I'm sorry Mister Crowther, but it must be family only. Rules,' the doctor had said.

More phone calls and passing the handset to the doctor confirmed that Barry was indeed willing to let Rob deal with the immediate issue.

Just before he left the hospital, at five am, a young nurse came scurrying up to him.

'Mister Crowther?' she asked.

'Yes?'

'I'll probably get wrong for this, but your mum said I should give you this before she… you know…'

She held in her hand the Aladdin's lamp from the panto.

Back home, after pouring himself a generous quarter pint of brandy into a large snifter and clipping the end from a cigar, Rob took the lid from the Aladdin lamp and cautiously looked inside.

He didn't really know what to expect, but he had half thought that there might be an ethereal blue light. There was nothing but dust.

He raised his glass to the dividing wall between the houses. 'Cheers, Lil,' he toasted, and downed half the liquid in one mouthful.

The bells were pealing and images of church steeples, yawning graves, undertakers and graveyards were squatting uninvited in Rob's mind, until he gradually realised that the 'bells' were in fact his phone ringing.

He opened his eyes and shifted uncomfortably in his clothes. He had spent the night on the settee after drinking almost a whole bottle of brandy.

'Y'mm…' he muttered into the phone.

'Mister Crowther?'

'Yeah.'

'Her Ladyship would be most obliged if you would attend the theatre

this morning,' a voice crackled.

'Wha'?' Rob replied rubbing his eyes, 'Wha' time 'sit?'

'I believe that it is almost noon, sir. Would you kindly bring the lamp with you.' The line went dead.

Rob let himself in through the same entrance that he and Lil had used the previous night but he went onto the stage area instead of front of house.

He fumbled in the soft glow of the emergency lights until he reached the control panel and tried to switch on the working lights. The only ones that came on were the blue show lights in the wings.

'I would have wished you a Merry Christmas, Mister Crowther,' stated an upper class female voice from the direction of the stage, *'but in the circumstances I shall wish you the compliments of the season.'*

'I shall second that,' stated a younger, male voice in the same clipped tone.

'Would you care to join us on stage?' asked the female.

Rob peered around the black serge leg and onto the stage area proper.

There, sitting on the rickshaw placed ready for Widow Twanky's entrance, was the shimmering shadow of a middle aged woman. Beside her stood a young man in his early twenties. They were both dressed as if they came from the nineteen-twenties or thirties.

'Er...' Rob started.

'Yes I know. It's somewhat disconcerting to be confronted by a couple of ghosts on Christmas Day...'

'Jacob Marley and all that,' interrupted the young man.

'Bertie!' scolded the woman.

'Sorry Mama.'

The woman regained her composure. *'As I was saying, to be confronted by a couple of ghosts on Christmas Day can be somewhat disconcerting. However, I should like to introduce you to several more, if I may?'*

Rob just nodded dumbly.

Five minutes later the stage seemed to be full of Harries and Georges and lift boys and Madam Secretaries and Julius and several more shadowy shapes.

'Finally,' stated the woman I shall introduce myself and my son. *'I am Lady Abigail Grey and this is my son, Bertie,'* she held out a hand to the male ghost, *'We were, unfortunately, killed when a lift plunged in its shaft in 1932.'* The ghost smiled. *'We all look after the place,'* she offered by way of explanation. *'Oh, and of course there is Doris. The poor dear girl was murdered up on the Grand Circle.'* she paused before calling, *'Doris?'*

A singular blue light seemed to float down from the flys and hover beside the head of the ghost that had been Lady Abigail Grey and hissed a whisper.

'Yes, I am sure that Mister Crowther has,' said Her Ladyship.

All the ghosts turned towards Rob.

'You did bring the lamp?' asked the woman.

Rob just nodded and withdrew the prop from beneath his jacket.

'If you would place it on stage please?'

Rob silently did as he was bid.

The ghosts then surrounded the lamp for a moment and then stepped away. In their midst was Lil, standing next to her sister.

'You have our full support, Mister Crowther, in your endeavours to rid this theatre of the unwanted,' stated Her Ladyship, *'and you may call on us at any time.'*

With that the whole of the ghostly enclave vanished and the white working lights flickered on.

'You are not going to believe me in a month of Sundays,' stated Rob, as he lay sprawled on his sofa, on the phone to Noodles.

'You do know that it's Christmas Day and that I intended to stop in bed until tea time,' replied the tech manager.

'Yeah, yeah… but you're not going to believe what I've got to say…'

'Rob. Jump in a cab. Come to mine. Food, drink, four o'clock. Tell me then. Christ, I can't even have a shag in peace!' and the line went dead.

'I do hope, Mister Royz, that you shall be keeping a close eye on Mister Crowther?'

'Assured, assured, your Ladyship. You may take it as read.'

'You are the only one of us that can venture outside of the theatre, because of your circumstances, and you must keep an eye on things.'

The Jewish ghost tipped a finger to his nineteenth century forelock: 'Assured, assured,' he repeated.

Jacob Royz had been one of several interred in the Temple Street graveyard, once outside the city walls, when the majority of the land had been acquired and the foundations laid for the theatre. In fact, it had been his skull that had been discovered when the renovation team had decided to revitalise the former picture house back into a theatre. He had not been pleased about the building work, not least because over time natural subsidence had separated his bones to the four compass points, leaving his head under the theatre, his ribcage somewhere between the two locations and his legs and feet in a courtyard between the buildings – where a Rabbi placed a stone on his grave every year..

He was, indeed, the only ghost that could venture outside the walls of the theatre and a fine time he could have if he weren't so *bored* by it all.

When the area had been governed by Yiddish tailors and wholesalers he could go abroad, surreptitiously suggesting various ploys to the retailers, but over the past few years the buildings had been pulled down – the hairdressers had been a favourite haunt – and rebuilt or transformed to be replaced by student accommodation, Asian shops, gay pubs, Chinese and Thai restaurants and burger bars. No one that wasn't of the Hebrew faith wanted a Jewish ghost offering advice, but now, well now he had a mission.

'Merry Christmas, Rob,' said the young, dark haired girl as he climbed from the cab outside Noodles flat. She then jumped nimbly into the back of the taxi and it sped off.

'Merry...' he started, but watched the black vehicle disappear down the street. He thought he may have recognised the departing female but made his way up the short garden path to the front door that was held slightly ajar by Noodles.

As the door opened fully Noodles, wearing just a towel, told him to go upstairs and make himself comfortable. 'I've opened a bottle of red,' he said as he followed Rob and then turned off the landing towards the bathroom.

Rob poured himself a glass of the wine and had just settled onto the multicoloured throw that covered the sagging settee when he realised who the girl was: one of the dancers from the show.

'Poured me one?' Noodles asked, appearing around the door now fully dressed.

'You do realise she's young enough to be your daughter?' Rob chided with a grin.

'Bollocks! She's twenty three,' Noodles grinned back, 'and what's so important as to drag me away from a carnal Christmas with a twirly?'

Over the bottle of wine Rob told Noodles about his late night and early morning experiences.

'If I didn't know you better, Crowther, I'd say you were full of shit,' admired Noodles. 'You take a dying woman into the theatre, then back to the hospital and then the lamp back to the theatre where you meet a pile of ghosts. Amazing. Not even you could make that up.'

'No stranger than a Persian statue causing havoc,' Rob stated. He downed the last mouthful of the red and wiggled the empty glass.

Noodles reached down beside the armchair and then, leaning over the arm of it, produced a large cardboard carton the contents of which clinked in a very pleasing manner.

'Chrissie pressie from mother,' he explained, 'white or red?'

'Red.'

'Open her up.' asked Noodles, 'I've got some stuff cooking. Back in a mo'.'

The Boxing Day shows were scheduled to be at one and four. However, because of poor sales – the consensus was that people were still stuffed with turkey and trimmings and were too full to travel into the metropolis – they had been cancelled.

Rob spent the first third of his day in bed reading, the next watching old movies on television and then decided to write down everything that had happened whilst it was still fresh in his mind.

He had just finished reading through the three pages of scribbled notes for the second time when his mobile phone rang.

'Hello?'

'You bored yet?' asked Dickie's voice.

'Off me tits'

'We're meeting in the Bodger at eight. Wanna come out and play?'

'We?'

'Me, Noodles, Foz.'

'See you there.'

The pub was packed, the juke-box was playing festive tunes at a reasonable level and there was a notice attached to the bar-flap that read:

"FOOD WILL BE STOP SERVICED FOR 30 'CLOCK TILL 3.30PM TODDY."

Someone on the bar staff had obviously had a seriously late night. It was equally obvious that the locals had decided that they were bored with repeats on television and screaming kids, and in-laws. The general mix was of people in their thirties and forties, with a few pensioners.

A lot of the crowd seemed to be alone but the majority were engaging in conversation with their neighbours.

After an hour of standing at one of the pedestal tables, the seating that the techies normally used became free and they slid into it.

Half an hour after that the pub seemed to rapidly empty.

'Was it something we said?' observed Foz, looking at the almost deserted space.

'Nah! Lot of people back at work tomorrow,' Noodles answered. 'and the Sound of Music will have finished by now. Same again?' he offered, waggling an empty pint glass.

At the bar, Dickie downed the last mouthful of lager, carefully placed the empty glass amongst several others and turned to Rob: 'Come on then, tell us?'

'What?'

'What you told Noodles yesterday,' was the reply.

Rob paused and took a deep breath. 'What's he said?'

'He said you'd seen the theatre ghosts,' Foz answered, 'all of them, on stage.'

At least, hoped Rob, Noodles hadn't said anything about Lil.

'Beers, Gents.' Noodles approached the table with four pints gripped in his hands and placed them carefully on the table.

Jacob Royz had been lurking behind the cash dispenser next to the techies table from the moment they had sat down. The problem was, because of the background music and the general hubbub of the customers, he couldn't hear what was being said. He had decided to do something about it, so using his post-death skills he had walked invisibly through the groups of punters, making them shudder, and suggesting to others, in an almost inaudible whisper, that it was time for home.

'That's better,' he thought, and settled back behind the machine.

'I just wanted a think after everyone had gone,' Rob explained, 'so I went back into the theatre and sat around… thinking. I didn't realise the time as I was…er…' he struggled for a moment, 'er, writing this.' He pulled the three sheets of notes from his breast pocket. 'Just everything that's happened.'

As he passed the notes onto the table he decided that he'd been wise to exclude the episode with Lil from his account.

'And that was it?' asked Foz, 'The ghosts just appeared?'

'I went on stage – I'd been sitting in the auditorium – and tried the lights but only the blues came on. That's when I saw them assembled on stage.'

'And you talked to them?' Dickie said after wiping his mouth of lager froth.

Rob nodded.

'And..?' everyone chorused.

'And they just said that they were worried about what was happening and that they would help me, us, get things back to normal.'

It was closing time when they were ready to leave the pub to make their way back to their various homes. As Rob stood up, slightly unsteadily, he remembered the three pages of, slightly soggy, notes still on the table. Folding them up he made to place them back into his breast pocket but missed, and the papers landed on the floor under the table. He didn't notice his mistake, and Foz was shouting from the doorway that the taxi was waiting to take them home.

Like an ethereal dervish, an almost invisible form darted from behind the cash machine and swept up the notes to waft them into a dark recess under the bench seating against the wall. Jacob Royz would read them later.

It was during the last scene of the first act that Rob, having finished his cues, made his way to the crew room and turned on the kettle. He glanced at the monitor that Stevie and his son had installed earlier that day; the picture hadn't changed. Two statues and an urn were still on top of the theatre roof.

They had some difficulty gaining access to the roof space for a second time as Tom was reluctant to go outside in the sleeting rain for a cigarette, so Noodles had simply asked for the key, with the excuse that the roof was leaking and he needed to see where from in case it interfered with the LX.

'I shouldn't really, you know. It's down to REAG to do that,' Tom complained as he handed over the key.

'Yeah right! I can just see that happening... oh... sometime never?'

The doorman nodded in agreement. 'You never got it from me,' he smiled.

As he poured hot water onto a tea bag a slight motion, from

the monitor, made Rob glance at it again. One of the statues was missing.

'Ah, shit!'

Seconds later Noodles' urgent voice over the Tannoy stated: 'Rob to flys, Rob to flys.'

He scaled the flights to the fly floor as if his tail was on fire, bursting through the door to find Stevie about to do his final cue of the act: bringing in the house curtain.

Rob shrugged and raised his hands towards Stevie but without saying a word.

As the big man pulled the brake on to hold the control rope he blurted excitedly, 'Y'll never effin guess what?'

'What?' Rob said, gasping for breath.

'I effin seen it. The dirty effin angel. It was up here. Red eyes and effin everything.'

'Where?'

'Sat on the end of the effin fly rail. It was just effin looking at me and then when I effin moved towards it it effed off in a cloud of effin dust to the grid!'

'You must have said something to Sam to get me up here?'

Stevie nodded, somewhat contritely. 'Sorry Rob. Didn't mean to effin panic you.'

'What made it fly off, do you think?'

'Dunno. But the eyes didn't half effin light up when I got near it. Just before it effin dissolved.'

Rob motioned Stevie towards the door: 'C'mon. Tea.'

Later that evening, in the Gods Bar, the lights were active again.

'You followed Mister Crowther, I understand?'

'I did Ma'am. Good job, too.'

'Oh? Explain what you mean Mister Royz?'

'He'd written down what you told me happened at Christmas. Dropped it in the public house up the road, he did.'

'I trust that you used your skills to retrieve the document?'

'Yes Ma'am. Very interesting it was too. I've a notion that I know what's happened.'

'Really? Do tell.'

'If you don't mind your Ladyship I'll just keep working at it until I'm certain.'

'Very well Mister Royz, very well.'

'Hello?' Rob had scrambled for the phone from a deep sleep.

'Rob? Noodles. Can you get down to the theatre for eleven? O'Leary's having a pow-wow. The professor and the writer are going to be there. I said you would as well.'

'Time 'sit?' Rob rubbed his eyes, still not awake.

'Half nine.'

''kay. I'll be there.'

He flipped the phone closed and laid his head back down on the still warm pillow. Why was it when you only had a seven o'clock evening show someone always threw in a spike, he wondered, and then leapt out of bed, splashed his face in the bathroom and, after dressing and gulping a cup of tea and smoking a cigarette, rang for a cab.

The taxi dropped him opposite the theatre entrance and just before he crossed to enter the foyer, he looked up to the top of the facade. The dirty angels were still guarding the urn.

As he entered the theatre Aggie looked up from one of the box office ticket terminals. 'Here for the meeting?' she asked.

Rob nodded.

'Upper Circle bar,' she told him, and went back to the computer. He made his way up the four flights of stairs and through the double doors into the marble and mirrored bar. It was still the same decor, albeit refreshed, as it had been when it was built in Victorian times.

In the middle of the floor there had been placed several of the heavy, square bar tables and seating had been placed around that. O'Leary, the comedy duo, Noodles and the Professor stood around chatting idly.

'Just Flynn to go,' Liddle noted as he saw Rob enter.

A few moments later the writer pulled open the door in a bit of a fluster, and immediately sat down, out of breath, 'Sorry, sorry, 'he apologised, 'the taxi was late and the traffic ridiculous. Sales. Huh!' he raised both eyebrows and clutched his satchel to his chest.

'Well, as we're all here,' O'Leary began, taking the initiative, 'we'll make a start.'

Seats were drawn up, people sat down.

'If I may make the opening?' asked Professor Vauxhall.

'By all means,' O'Leary answered.

'Whilst I was up in Northumberland I managed to do some more research and to contact some fellows in the States that are also working on the tracts. As I may have mentioned, the words that I've been working on were found in Persia but they are of Moghreb origin; Moghreb meaning "western" or "sunset" in Arabic. They were the peoples that inhabited the three countries between the high areas of the Atlas Mountains and the Mediterranean Sea. Historically, some writers have also included Spain and Malta in the definition. But I digress. Erm, yes, they were very interested in what has transpired,' he continued, and as an aside, 'I actually had an email from the Department of Homeland Security.' He cleared his throat. 'Anyway, some of my colleagues agreed with your premise that it could possibly be an incantation that I mistakenly gave to Mister Forbins.'

'Sorry?' apologised the writer, 'I'm somewhat confused – I thought we were here to talk about the … my … situation … that had… er… arisen front of house?'

Vauxhall looked between O'Leary and Forbins but, not getting an answer to his questioning look, he continued, 'I gave, in good faith, what I thought was a translation asked for by your writer. However, as I had been somewhat engaged since the early hours of the morning, I gave the word for "statue" instead of "stone" – "altmtheil" not "ahjar" – a simple mistake... as it is written in an early form of Phoenician.'

The writer was on his feet: 'What are you talking about? What is going on..?'

'Sit down please, Flynn,' suggested O'Leary calmly, 'it will all become clear very shortly.'

The writer sat back down.

'Please give us your update, Noodles,' asked the producer.

'I think Rob can do a better job actually...' the tech manager turned to his friend.

Rob half stood and placed his fingertips on the table: 'Before I start, can I just ask Flynn if he has his diary with him?'

The writer reached into his satchel and pulled out the book. 'I always do.'

'What did you write yesterday – about lunch time?'

'I don't think I...' he paused to flick pages, 'I just wrote "theatre what?" He then held open the page and presented it to the company. 'Why?'

'Do you know what happened here during the first show yesterday?' Rob quizzed.

'How could I? I was at home.'

'Did you write anything today about this meeting?'

'No. I... What is this? I shall not be interrogated in this manner!' He made to stand.

Rob beat him to his feet by pulling himself upright: 'Please Flynn, just bear with me.' He went to the bar and rang the stage door extension. It was answered almost immediately.

'Stevie? ... Yeah, go to the monitor and if anything happens in the next five minutes bell me back up here.' Rob had the foresight, whilst travelling in the cab to the theatre, to ring Stevie, as he lived the closest to the venue, to get to work before his time call and to wait beside the phone. 'Yeah … Upper Circle Bar … 223.' He replaced the handset.

'Just pander to me for a few moments more, Flynn, please.' Rob held out a pen that he had taken from his pocket. 'On today's page, please write the same as you did yesterday.'

The author took the pen and scrawled the message. Handing back the pen he asked, 'Now what?'

'Now we wait a few moments.'

They didn't have long to wait until the phone chirruped and started to ring.

'Yeah?' was all Rob said before nodding and putting down the receiver.

'Well?' asked Forbins and all eyes were upon Rob.

'He wrote. It moved.'

'For God's sake, will someone please explain what is going on!' screeched the writer.

He listened for half an hour and pooh-poohed everything that was put to him until Rob asked him to read from the diary once more as he cross referenced the events that had occurred in the theatre with the playwright's entries.

'You cannot attribute the blame for this to me!' Forbins finally said as he made to stand up again. 'I shan't take any responsibility for something that *he* told me.' he pointed an accusing finger at Vauxhall.

'No one is blaming anyone,' stated Bigg.

'No one,' confirmed Liddle.

That seemed to calm the writer slightly.

'What we have is a problem of no one's making,' confirmed the Professor. 'It has happened and we need to sort it out before someone has a serious accident.'

'"Shit happens",' quoted Rob, 'we just don't want it to get any deeper. If I might suggest that you don't write *anything* pertaining to the panto in that?' He pointed to the journal that was open at the last entry. 'Or even anything about the theatre.'

'No, no, of course not,' the writer assured him, trembling slightly.

Noodles tapped Rob on the shoulder and pointed to his watch.

'Time for lunch?' suggested O'Leary, with an encouraging smile.

Noodles nodded.

'Then let us take ourselves off to the pub where we can all have a drink and ponder on what has been said.'

No one had noticed the small blue light that had hovered throughout the meeting between the whisky and the gin behind the bar.

The Jew and the gentry met, briefly, on the back stairs from the Upper Circle bar.

'*You are closer to finding out about this thing that has appeared, Mister Royz?*'

'*I think so, Your Ladyship. I just need to confirm a few things that I have learned in the past hour, or so.*'

'*Very good. You will keep me informed?*'

'*Assuredly… and then we need to see Mister Crowther.*'

'*Rather, a case of his seeing us?*' Bertie grinned.

After the lunchtime meeting, during which Forbins had mellowed having imbibed almost two bottles of red wine but no food, the gathering broke up. The actors went their separate ways and the Professor returned to the University to research more on the Moghreb and to see if any email had come down the line from colleagues. Rob and Noodles went back to the stage door with Stevie, who had joined them for a couple of pints.

Back in the crew room they inspected the monitor. The statue had returned to its position.

'I didn't like t'effin say anything in the pub,' Stevie admitted, 'but I know what scares the effin thing.'

Both Noodles and Rob's heads snapped to the speaker.

The fly man nodded, ''least ways, I think I do.'

'Spill the beans, then' asked Noodles.

Stevie took off his denim jacket, revealing bare arms and a tee-shirt, and hung it on a peg over the radiator. 'This.' He pointed to a tattoo on his arm.

'What? A tat of a heart with your kids' names on it?' Rob asked, incredulously.

'Eh? Oh, sorry.' He moved his hand down a few inches. 'This.' He indicated an inky black cross with a loop at the top.

'An ankh?'

'Used to be a effin "Kiss" fan back in the effin early eighties,' grinned Stevie, pulling at the bottom of the washed-out tee-shirt to stretch Vinnie Vincent's face, the one-time guitarist with the group.

'He's got the same thing painted on his face,' Noodles observed, 'sure it wasn't the face that did it?' he mocked.

'Yeah, yeah. That's why I effin think that's what effin did it.'

'Sorry Stevie, you lost me somewhere along the line. Explain?' Rob apologised as he filled the kettle.

The redhead took a deep breath. 'When you rung me I saw the effin thing sort of... dissolve. The way it did up on the effin fly floor. So I thought I'd go and see where it was. Found the effin thing on the Gods and tried to sneak up on it.'

'That was a bit daft after what happened to Simone.' Rob retorted.

Stevie shrugged. 'Anyway the thing must have effin heard me and flaps off down the back stone stairs to the effin fire exit. No effin way out. Doors are chained and me a couple of effin feet away when it turns to look at me… red eyed and everything…'

'And?'

'Y' ever seen a bit of stone effin panic?' Stevie pulled up his tee-shirt to reveal a large, blackening bruise on his left breast.

The seven o'clock show came and went without incident until curtain down.

'Would Mister O'Leary please contact the F - O - H as soon as he is out of his costume please,' rang Sam's voice over the Tannoy.

No one thought anything of it until five minutes later when O'Leary's voice crackled onto the same public address. 'Would all company members and crew please make their way to stage immediately!' was all that was said, but with a sense of urgency.

'What effin now?' asked Stevie as he pulled on his jacket.

'Fuck knows, Mate,' Dickie replied on his way out of the door.

A few moments later the whole company was assembled on stage under the fluorescent working lights and Dan O'Leary was waiting for silence before he spoke. A heavy-set man in a large overcoat was standing with him, his blond hair slick from the adverse weather outside.

'I'm afraid that I have some bad news for everyone,' O'Leary said. 'Our writer, Mister Flynn Forbins, has been found stabbed.

'This is D.I. Keiths who would like to ask a few questions.' He motioned towards the damp policeman.

'Sorry to break this news, folks, but at around eight o'clock this evening the writer of your panto was found in a toilet cubicle in the Central Station with multiple stab wounds… he's been taken to the Victoria Hospital.'

A gasp was heard from several members of the cast.

'…We understand that he conversed with some of you today and also had lunch with some of you. Mister O'Leary has told me about those. If anyone spoke to Mister Forbins today I would like them to stay behind so that my officers in the auditorium can take statements. Thank you.'

'I bet that was a bundle of fun?' observed Dickie sardonically as Rob, Noodles and Stevie returned from the bar having just managed last orders after their interviews and statements, and joined them at the usual table.

'Poor fucker pegged it,' Rob stated, 'just as we were coming round here.'

'Morder!' stated Tam.

'Yup! The coppers are looking at the CCTV stuff,' Noodles replied before taking a sup of his beer.

'What worries me is that whoever stiffed him took his stuff. Satchel, wallet, watch. If somebody writes in that diary...' Rob left the rest unsaid.

'Least we've got some defence,' Stevie stated, pointing at his tee-shirt.

The crew fell silent for a moment and were slightly startled when Noodles blurted: 'Pickpocket!'

'Eh? What's that effin got to do with it?'

'Remember a good few years ago, Rob, somebody lifted your wages down in Billy's bar and a couple of hours later the hotel opposite the station rang to say they'd found your wallet in a rubbish skip?'

Rob nodded whilst taking a mouthful of his pint.

'What do you bet we'll find whatever the mugger didn't want in the same place?'

After finishing their beer Rob and Noodles left the pub and walked down the almost empty street just as the icy rain became even heavier, crossed a junction and made their way down a narrow lane towards the station. However, before crossing the road they turned left, past the hotel entrance, and left again to go through a darkened gateway into a yard full of hotel detritus. Beyond that were six large cylindrical skips, brimming with rubbish.

Both of them reached for their MagLite torches to inspect whatever they could find.

It was a mere two or three moments later when Noodles cried, 'Rob, satchel!' he pointed behind one of the skips. 'Better ring the law.'

Rob was dog tired having repeated his story three or four times to D.I. Keiths – as probably had Noodles, who was in another interview room somewhere in the same Police Station – and provided his fingerprints.

Eventually, a uniform had held the door open and told him that he could go home. Noodles and he shared a taxi in near silence.

'My feet are friggin' killing me,' Rob grumbled, feeling the leaden weight of his steel toe-capped boots on each foot.

'It's my arse that's doing me in. Those cop shop chairs are none too comfortable.'

After dropping Noodles at his flat Rob went home and poured himself a large brandy before slumping into an armchair and easing off his work boots. Both socks had holes in the toes, and as he peeled them off they stuck to his skin where his feet had been bleeding slightly.

'The joy of theatre,' he grimaced.

The news of Forbins' murder was the talk of the theatre next day as well as being plastered across the local television and printed news.

When Rob's cab turned up at the theatre he could see that there were several reporters and photographers, together with a TV crew, assembled outside the foyer. A lone hack hovered at the stage door in Rob's path.

When asked for a comment Rob just walked past the reporter and into Tom's domain.

'The vultures are circling,' Tom stated, looking up from his local newspaper. 'Dan and the other two came in the back way. Can you go see him?'

Rob nodded and headed for the crew room to drop off his jacket and the carrier bag that held his boots; he'd elected to wear a pair of trainers that he had found lurking in the bottom of the wardrobe until the boots were needed.

Crossing the stage and entering the backstage corridor he made his way to dressing room one and knocked three times in quick succession.

The door was opened by O'Leary's wife, Chrissie.

'Morning Rob!' Come in,' invited the actor.

The door closed silently.

'You've heard?'

'Forbins dying? Yes, of course'

'No, no. About Noodles.'

'Noodles? Why? What's happened?' blurted Rob, slightly panicked.

'Ah, then you haven't. Fell downstairs in his flat this morning… broken leg.'

'Ahhh… shit!'

'Exactly. It means I want you in charge until we can sort him out.'

Rob thought for a moment and then commented, 'Nothing to do with the statue…?'

The actor shook his head, 'I wouldn't think so.'

'Okay. Anything I need to know?'

'We'll have to shuffle the cues around. If you can get your guys together and sort that out? Give them what you do and then see

Sam. I'm sure you know what Noodles does?'

'Sort of,' he replied.

'Okay, well, see Sam, okay?'

Chrissie O'Leary silently opened the door.

On the way back to the crew room Rob muttered, 'Three shows back-to-back and I'm in at the deep end. Oh joy.'

'That's going to fuck things up,' was Foz's comment on hearing the news of Noodles' accident and that all the cues were to be shuffled. 'I mean… y'know… cues are like Xmas parcels. You know when to deliver them.'

As soon as Sam arrived Rob joined her in prompt corner and went through "the book" – the script of the panto showing where the cues go – and scribbled down the cues that she knew about, and then inserted the ones that she didn't know – like paging the on-stage door so that the young dancers, the babes, could get on and off stage safely.

'Ladies and gentlemen this is your Act One beginners' call,' warned the Tannoy just as Rob returned to the crew room.

'Bollocks!' he stated and immediately turned round and went to the stage door for a cigarette, knowing that he had five minutes before the curtain went up if all the patrons were in their seats.

'Two effin down and one to effin go. Didn't go too effin badly.'

'Hmm. Maybe not for you, Stevie, but I fucked up on the first one,' Rob admitted, 'bloody doubled up with a trap cue. Sorry guys,' he apologised.

They waved the apology aside.

'Bound to happen,' Harley remarked, turning the page of his new motorcycle magazine.

'I thought we were getting something to eat during this break?' groused Dickie.

'Bloody right,' Tam agreed, 'Ah cud eat a scabby arsed horse.'

'I'll go and look in the Green Room,' said Rob heading out the door, 'It's probably all been delivered there.'

'Ef its pizza – like last year – make sure y' gets a pepperoni!' Tam called after Rob's departing back.

Crossing the stage Rob could hear the next crowd of punters through the drapes; there was an excited buzz as they started to take their seats. Half an hour and another show – pizza would sit like a lead weight.

'So, Mister Royz, you believe that you know what it is and how to remedy the situation?'

'I do, Ma'am. But we shall have to speak to Mister Crowther,'

'Very well. I shall leave initial contact up to you.'

'Yes, Ma'am.'

O'Leary pulled on a long, dark silk, dressing gown before passing through the front of house curtain to face the audience in the glow of the footlights.

He was met with applause, but he subdued it by flattening his hands and making downward motions for quiet.

'Boys and Girls, Ladies and Gentlemen,' he announced solemnly, 'as you may know our writer met with an unfortunate mishap last evening, as he was leaving the theatre.' He paused whilst the audience muttered. 'This evening's show is dedicated to his memory. Thank you.' He shuffled back through the curtain, to loud applause, and threw the robe into the wings and said, 'Sam! When you're ready.'

She hit the "standby" switches, flicked the green "go" for the orchestra and the production started with the usual timpani roll and crash.

After the show they all assembled in the Bodger, but Rob was in no mood for company. For one he wanted to know how Noodles was, and secondly his feet were still aching – even more so after the days running around sans steelies.

After only one pint he announced, 'I'm off home, lads. See you at twelve tomorrow,' and then jumped into a waiting taxicab.

Just as the cab was about to pull away, Dickie thumped on the window and held up a carrier bag.

'Hold it, mate!' Rob instructed the driver and wound down the window.

'Nearly forgot these,' said Dickie, passing across the carrier bag that held his boots, 'see y' t'morrow.'

On the fifteen minute drive to his place Rob could feel his eyelids starting to droop and realised that he not eaten all day; as soon as he got through the front door he dropped the bag beside the settee and pulled a ready meal from the freezer. Lasagne would do.

Slamming the plastic tray into the microwave he made his way upstairs, undressing as he did so, and turned on the shower in the bathroom. Ten minutes later he heard the tell tale 'ping' that said his meal actually was ready.

Slipping on just his tee-shirt and jeans he made his way to the kitchen, ripped the film from the meal and started to eat it with a soup spoon as he walked back into the living room. Just before he lowered himself onto the settee, supper in hand, he turned on the television for the late local news.

It was all about Forbins and they showed a grainy CCTV picture of a suspect, who was believed to be a heroin user according to "Police Sources".

The meal and the news finished, he poured himself the now

customary large brandy and thought about lighting up a cigar.

He realised that he must have nodded off when he looked at the clock and it told him it was five past twelve. He was now wide awake.

'Bollocks!' he exclaimed exasperated and reached for the brandy, a cigar and the cutter after turning off the television.

He had only taken a few draws on the stogie when a voice behind him asked, *'Is that good tobacco, Mister Crowther?'*

Rob half choked on smoke and dropped his brandy snifter into his groin spilling the contents. 'Wha…!' he exclaimed as he looked around.

'I'm sorry, I didn't mean to scare you; it's just that I do like a good cigar.'

Rob, still coughing slightly, managed to utter, 'Who the fuck's there?'

'Oh, sorry. I do forget sometimes.'

With that, a mist-like swirl ascended from the carrier bag, which Rob had dropped earlier and developed into a blue transparent figure of a long-bearded man dressed in a dark suit and wearing a cap.

As he made a slight bow the figure said: *'Jacob Royz. Her Ladyship's compliments.'*

'Her Ladyship? You mean you're one of the theatre ghosts?'

'Seconded for the duration. Adopted if you like. I do apologise for spilling your drink.'

'How come you're here and not in the theatre?'

'Ah! Long story – with which I shall not bore you – suffice to say that I am the only one who can leave those environs.'

Rob eyed the apparition suspiciously as he dabbed at his groin with a handkerchief taken from his back pocket.

'May I sit?' asked the ghost.

Rob held out one hand to indicate the fireside armchair and poured a replacement brandy with the other.

The ghost seemed to sink into the seat and then, finding the correct level, hovered just above the cushion. It crossed its legs.

'*Very comfortable,*' it observed. '*It is a long time since I had the opportunity to rest in someone's parlour.*'

'I hope you're not going to make a habit of it,' Rob stated, 'scared the shit out of me you did.'

'*Yes. As I said, I'm sorry.*'

'How did you get here? The carrier I suppose?'

'*Actually, no... sort of. I've been waiting inside your left boot since the last show came down. You nearly forgot the bag and unless I'd had a quiet word with your colleague this conversation would have had to be postponed.*'

'You spoke to Dickie..?'

'*Whispered a suggestion, shall we say.*'

'You seem to have all the bases covered Mister Royz.' Rob took a sip of his brandy, which had warmed up. 'What can I do for you?'

'*I don't begin to understand the first part of your comment but the second...*' the ghost shrugged, '*... it's not what you can do for me, rather what I can do for you.*'

Rob raised an eyebrow.

'*I shall come straight to the point. Do you know what a golem is?*'

'Er... Tolkien, deformed Hobbit, eats fish, covets ring,' Rob summarised, somewhat perplexed.

'*No, no. Not a Goll-um; a go-lem,*' the ghost shrugged again, '*although I believe that is a very good story – according to Doris.*'

Rob had to admit that he didn't know what a "golem" was.

The apparition removed its hat to reveal that he was wearing a kippuh, a skullcap, and dropped the held headgear towards the floor where it floated about an inch from the carpet.

'*Let me explain.*' it started.

After over an hour of Judaic and Moghreb history, two cigars, a few brandies and several questions, Rob eventually realised that he had been sitting on the edge of his seat, so he sat back against the cushions.

'So, let me get this right, what you are saying is that a golem is a clay figure that has had life breathed into it and that is what we've got sitting on the roof?'

Jacob Royz shrugged and spread his hands: *'Hmm. After a fashion.'*

'Stevie reckons that he scared it today with an ankh.'

The ghost started to laugh so hard that visible tears rolled down its cheeks and into its beard.

What's so funny?' Rob asked.

'My dear boy,' Jacob Royz said, *'it wasn't the ankh that scared it – it was the name.'*

'What?' Rob asked trying to recall the tee-shirt, 'Vinney?'

'Not so much "Vinney" as the two ens. In Hebrew the symbol for "dead" is the symbol for "truth" – less one letter. As I explained earlier "Emet" is written on the forehead of a golem to bring it to life.'

'Sorry?'

'Emet means truth, met means dead. The golem obviously saw the two ens. Do you have writing material?'

Rob scrambled on the table to find a piece of paper and a pen. He found paper and a pencil.

'Lay one on top of the other,' instructed the ghost.

Rob did as he was bid and suddenly the pencil took on a life of its own with a slight blue glow. It started to write.

"תמא"

'That is the word for truth.' stated Jacob.

"תמ"

'And that, the one for death.'

Rob stared at what the pencil had written until it dropped lifeless onto the paper. 'Good job that guitarist wasn't called "Vixnney".' he stated, staring at the ghost.

The ghost smiled, briefly and then said: *'If he had been, your friend would be very dead.'*

'So what do we do about it? How do we get rid of it?' Rob asked, as he started to clip yet another cigar.

'Ah!' stated the ghost, 'now there's the rub.'

Rob awoke on the settee at just after six the next morning. The room smelt of stale cigars but there was no sign of Jacob Royz. He pondered about what the ghost had told him the previous night and thought, for a minute perhaps, that he had dreamt it – until he saw the paper with the symbols on it.

He stumbled barefoot into the kitchen and made a cup of strong tea.

'Noodles,' he thought and went back into the living room and took the mobile phone from his jacket. Dialling operator services he asked for the number of the "A & E" and to be put through.

After several diversions – one of which stumped him as he couldn't remember Noodles' real Christian name – he was eventually put through to the correct ward, the correct bed and the correct patient.

'If you'd been pissed you'd never have broken it!' exclaimed Rob when Noodles answered the phone.

'Probably,' replied Noodles, somewhat disconsolately.

'How're you doing?'

'Oh y' know. Sat here twiddling me thumbs wondering about the show and you know what.'

'Never you mind about the show. Dan's asked me to look after it. As for "you know what" I met someone last night that can help.'

'Yeah?'

'Yeah. I'll tell you about it when I see you.'

The conversation continued for another few moments, about treatment and the bonny state of the nurses, until they said goodbye and Rob returned to his tea.

'You could have introduced me.' whined an irate voice from the carrier bag.

Rob dropped the cupful of hot tea and the scream could possibly have been heard in the theatre.

'Two today; one tomorrow and then off for two days,' Foz stated, rubbing his hands together with glee. 'You doing anything for New Years, Rob?'

'Nah. Thought I might go and keep Noodles company.'

'Bummer that,' Stevie joined the conversation, 'Broke in two effin places and he needs it effin screwing together. He's going to be off a long effin time.'

'Which is why…' Rob started, pulling a cotton cash-bag from his pocket, 'we're going to have a whip-round.' He pulled a ten pound note from his other pocket and pushed it into the bag. Everyone else in the crew room followed suite and then Rob took the bag to Sam and explained what was happening.

'Nice gesture, Rob,' she said, also pushing a tenner into the sack, 'I'll send it round the dressing rooms.'

'Thanks, Sam.'

In the interval of the second show Rob was standing at the trough urinal going about the usual business and trying to push the blue sani-block towards the sump.

'*Her Ladyship requests your presence this evening,*' said Julius' voice behind him.

Rob jumped and sprayed his boots. 'I wish your lot would announce yourselves with a little more consideration.'

'*Gods Bar.*'

He was sure he heard echoing laughter – although it could have been the plumbing.

When the show was about to come down Rob made sure that he was standing beside the prompt desk for the final cue.

'Stand by tabs,' warned Sam over the headset.

The call was acknowledged by Stevie.

'Tabs… Go!'

The final walk-down had gone without incident and also the spiel that O'Leary had given about "… and if you enjoyed the show then come back next year when we're doing Sleeping Beauty."

'If anyone wants me, Sam, I'll be front of house. Just going to sort something out.'

The girl nodded and continued scribbling notes.

The emergency lights cast a deathly pallor throughout the Gods Bar – it hadn't been used for years and the old pool table showed signs of the roof above it where slates had leaked years of rainwater or melting snow into the void above and dripped down.

The lights in the street below added to the feeling of loneliness as they glowed orange through the yellowing net curtains.

Rob sat on a bench seat under the arched window, and waited.

The lights in the overhead chandelier suddenly started to glow faintly and then to grow to their full brightness. They then dimmed and flashed twice.

Is that more of a warning, Rob?' asked Julius' voice from somewhere above his head.

He looked up to the stained tongue and groove wooden ceiling but couldn't see where the voice had come from.

'Good evening Mister Crowther,' said Her Ladyship, who was perched on the rim of the pool table; she swung her ankle-length dress into place. *'Mister Julius suggested that we announce ourselves in a*

more appropriate fashion after your... surprise ... of earlier.'

'Yeah, well, he always did have a habit of lurking in the most unexpected places,' Rob commented.

Her Ladyship got straight to the point: *'I understand that you had a rather protracted conversation with Mister Royz the other evening?'*

'Yeah. Learned quite a bit.' he nodded. 'Golems and such.'

'Indeed. However I understand that this thing is not a golem, Jewish as such, but is somewhat earlier?'

'Jacob Royz suggests Phoenician.'

'Then if I may make a suggestion, Mister Crowther, I think that you need to see a Jewish Saturday car.'

'Er... sorry..?'

The ghost smiled. *'Mister Royz will not mind I am sure but there is a joke about a Jewish Saturday car that I learned from Bertie, who heard it in the music halls...'*

'Yeah?'

Her Ladyship cleared her throat as if about to give a eulogy. *'What kind of car does a Jew drive on a Saturday?'* she asked.

Rob stepped into the spirit of the old joke. 'I don't know, Your Ladyship. What kind of a car does a Jew drive on a Saturday?'

If a ghost could have blushed then surely this one would have.

'He doesn't.' she replied, giggling. *'He vaux all the vay there...'*

'And he vaux all the vay back,' finished Rob.

'Oh! You've heard it?'

'Sorry Your Ladyship, but that was old when Adam was a lad and in these days of political correctness – and "health and safety" garbage – stuff like that is about as welcome as a pain in the... tukis.'

'Oh dear, well in that case will you please see Professor Vauxhall and tell him of the findings that Mister Royz gave you. I am sure that, as a very learned academic, he will be able to help us.'

Knowing that he had to be in the theatre for noon the next day, Rob rang the Professor as soon as his meeting in the Gods' Bar had finished and arranged to meet him in the burger bar at the top of the main shopping street at ten the next morning.

It was now a quarter past ten; the academic was late, so Rob ordered another Styrofoam cup of what the place called tea and retook his seat. As he sipped the dispiritingly less than hot liquid he stared out of the window at the street.

What was it Billy S. had once written? "The world's a stage…" – or some such? Well if the life out there was theatre, then God help theatre.

Suits with mobile phone Bluetooth earpieces; students texting; barely-in-their-teens mothers pushing buggies in which sat kids enjoying that essential induction to a lifetime's bad eating, the sucked and sickly sausage roll; chavs either drunk, stoned or on the way there; pensioners that were gaunt and dead-eyed. It was Faust in all its hideousness.

'Can I clear the table, Mister?' asked a mousy-haired girl of about sixteen or seventeen who was chewing gum as she swabbed the tables with a too-wet cloth.

Rob, turning away from the streetscape to face her, stared and muttered: 'Was this the face that launched a thousand chips?' and nodded.

'Eh?'

'Sorry…' he glanced at her name badge that bore a single star – of a possible five – and grinned. '…Helen.' He moved his elbows from the surface.

'Morning Rob,' said the familiar voice of Professor Vauxhall sliding into a seat with a cup of what promised, idly, to be coffee. 'Sorry I'm late; I was waiting for a call.'

'Morning Professor.'

The girl collected two empty styro-cups and gave a cursory wipe with her non-too-clean cloth to the laminate table top leaving it streaked with a fine patina of grease.

'I understand, from what you said on the phone, that there have been some developments,' the academic stirred a sachet of sugar into the coffee.

'I've been talking to a… er, friend of the theatre who has some knowledge of Moghreb and Jewish history.'

'Really? Do I know him?'

'I would say not, he comes from a fair distance away,' stated Rob, and it went through his mind that 1852 was indeed a fair way away. 'He thinks that we have what is the forerunner of a golem – and the Tolkien joke has been done.'

The Professor took a sip of his coffee and twisted his face: 'Gods, but that's awful.' He replaced the lid on the cup and pushed it away. 'I suppose you think it's too early for a proper drink?'

Rob grinned. 'I'm awake,' was all he said.

'Good. There's a pub down by the market that opens at nine.' He slid from the bench seat to stand up. 'Shall we?'

It only took them a few minutes to walk through the shopping centre and exit down some stairs to the 'Black Garter'.

As they entered, an almost toothless and ancient woman, dressed in a black fur hat and Astrakhan overcoat, sidled up to the Professor. 'Long time no see Prof,' she mumbled, 'you doin' more research?'

'Hello, Bea,' he smiled, 'no, just out for a drink.'

As she wandered off into the crowded bar she raised her schooner of dark liquid and said, 'anytime… anytime.'

'I did a bit of research into the language of market traders some time ago; she was invaluable,' Vauxhall explained to Rob, who nodded and pushed his way to the bar.

'What'll it be?'

'A brandy, please. Large one.'

Within moments the barmaid, a white-haired Irish woman in her sixties, had filled Rob's pint and served the brandy, adeptly fulfilling a couple of other orders at the same time.

Rob looked around for the Professor and found him sitting at a table in the corner of the bar. Several people were standing next to the academic's table; he seemed to know them, and was chatting and smiling. As Rob placed the drinks the assembled market traders, he assumed, drifted away.

'Now,' started the Professor, 'you were saying?'

'Yeah. Golem. What do you know about them?'

'Made from clay; Jewish folk-law; Rabbi Judah Loew the Maharal of Prague, created one to defend the ghetto of Josefov, y'know, when the Emperor decreed that all the Jews were to be killed…'

'Okay, but the actual thing? What do you know about that?' Rob sipped from his pint.

The Professor shrugged.

Someone at the other side of the bar started to play what Rob recognised as Charlie Musselwhite's "Skinney Woman" on the Blues harmonica.

'Jimmy! Shouted the barmaid in an accent straight from the Falls Road, 'W' don't have a feckin music loicence, so shut th' feck up!'

The gob iron stopped as suddenly as it had started.

Rob grinned as the Professor stated: 'That's what I like about this place. Proper pub.' He took a large mouthful of his brandy.

'I learned from this friend that the statue on the roof may be a golem,' Rob took another mouthful of beer, 'and that they are animated by writing "emet" on their forehead…'

'The Yiddish for "truth"?'

'Yeah. And to kill them you simply wipe out the "e" leaving "met" – which means dead.'

'But we're dealing with something pre-Judaic here. How is that going to help?'

'Phoenician, my friend reckons.'

The academic nodded sagely. 'That would make sense. The Phoenicians were very prolific around the Mediterranean and that area. I should like to meet your friend, he seems very knowledgeable.'

'Can you look into this?' Rob asked, ignoring the academic's request.

'Of course, of course. This thing has obviously got to be stopped. With the death of Forbins it may start to think for itself and then all hell could break loose. Another pint?'

Rob accepted the offer.

'Jeez I used to drink fifteen pints in a day,' Rob thought as he washed his face in cold water in the crew toilet, 'five and I'm pissed these days.' The session with the academic had turned into a meeting of old pals when some more of the market traders had turned up and Bea had rejoined them.

Rob had managed to escape as the Professor was onto his seventh large brandy. The alcohol seemed to have no effect on him.

He took a deep breath. 'Okay, Crowther, work head,' he looked at himself in the mirror over the sink. 'Work head,' he repeated.

The fluorescent tube on the ceiling flickered.

He took another deep breath: 'Yes Julius?'

'After the show Jacob Royz would like to see you in the Gods.' said the voice from the cistern.

'Okay.' Rob splashed more of the cold water onto his face.

'Y' know I wus thinkin',' stated Tam, just before the start of the show.

'This could be dangerous,' noted Dickie.

'Ah wis thinkin' aboot th' beastie on th' roof,' the Scot continued, ignoring his workmate, apart from flipping him a couple of fingers, 'and came t' th' conclusion tha' i' didnae bother us on a Saturday show.'

'And so?' asked Rob.

'Dunno. It jist didnae.'

'Keep thinking, Tam,' Harley suggested.

'Beginners to stage. Beginners to stage, please.' stated the Tannoy.

Rob waited for the lights to come on, or at least flicker. Eventually they did.

'Mem he taw' said the voice of Jacob Royz.

'Sorry?' replied Rob, looking around the deserted bar area.

The shade of the Jew appeared, sitting on a bench seat opposite Rob.

'That's the Phoenician phrase that you need to use to get rid of our problem,' and he repeated: *'"Mem he taw".'*

'And how do you propose that I use this phrase?'

'We suggest that you speak to your Professor friend. Actually, he's having a drink in the pub as we speak.'

As Rob left the theatre by the front doors, a quicker way out than taking the circuitous route to the stage door, he wondered if the Professor was in any way sober enough to understand what Rob was going to tell him.

He could hear the noise from the pub as he left the theatre having asked Aggie to ring the stage door to record that he'd gone out this way.

The Bodger was packed to the doors – people were in party mood already even though New Year was still two days away.

As he pushed and excused his way to the bar he noticed Foz and the rest of the crew sitting at their usual table. Foz had obviously been keeping an eye out for him as he motioned drinking, with a wiggled cupped palm to his mouth, and pointed to the table.

Did that mean that Foz wanted a drink or that there was a drink waiting for him? He frowned and shrugged.

Foz held up a pint of Guinness and pointed at Rob.

'Good man', thought Rob grinning, 'he's got the beers in,' as he pressed further through the crowd to the table.

Foz passed Rob his pint, over the heads of those seated at the table, and then made a space so that Rob could squeeze in.

'Thought you might need that after your "meeting",' Foz nodded.

Rob took a deep drink before answering. 'Short meeting. Don't suppose you've seen the Professor anywhere?'

'He's just nipped to the loo. Shouldn't be too long.'

'Not pissed is he?' asked Rob, thankful that he didn't have to scour the pub for him.

'Not a bit. He's drinking mineral water or something,' pointing out a half full glass at the other end of the table. 'Been to the show, he says.'

Another mouthful of Guinness later and the academic returned to the table pushing his way through to rejoin the crew. He had obviously been talking to Dickie and Tam as the three seemed to resume a conversation that Rob couldn't hear over the hubbub.

Glancing up from his drink the Professor noticed Rob looking at him, smiled and raised his glass.

Rob returned the compliment and also made a sign for wanting to talk; then pointed towards the toilets.

The academic gave a querying look, held up a hand and then three fingers in a gesture of acknowledgement but to give him that number of minutes.

Ron downed his pint and then pushed out into the crowd again; it would take two minutes to get to the gents.

'I shouldn't be doing this,' Billy stated, as he crawled along the metal beam that was rigged with pyrotechnics. His body harness was chafing in all the wrong places; it had been a very long day and he had hardly managed to slip out of it.

'What?' crackled a voice in his earpiece.

'Sorry mate, just thinking out loud.'

'Can you see the firing relay?'

'Yeah, yeah. Nearly there. It's got a red instead of a green. Be fixed in a minute.' Billy reached into his shoulder-strapped tool pouch and withdrew a screwdriver before turning his comms set off.

High above the river, on a cold piece of steel, Billy Marchant, pyrotechnical technician, did what he had to do for the next night's firework display. At midnight the whole Quayside and the surrounding area would echo to the sound of bangs, cracks, explosions and everything else that went with the pyro display for the New Year. Just now, though, he was cold. 'Tea and a wee', he thought, 'that's what I need.'

The firing mechanism test button pressed, and the green light glowing, Billy pressed his comms button.

After a short crackle a voice said, 'All done?'

'Yeah. Can I go to the pub now?'

'We both can mate,' came back the reply, 'mind how you come down.'

'Yeah, yeah,' Billy replied wearily as his foot slipped and without noticing he nudged one of the large fireworks and some cabling out of position.

'Mem-he-taw,' Rob pronounced again, his voice echoing slightly within the tiled toilet that held the usual trough and four cubicles.

'And where did you find this out?' Professor Vauxhall asked as he buttoned his fly after relieving himself.

'The... er... internet,' Rob lied.

'Mem-he-taw?' the Professor repeated, 'Phoenician, unless I'm mistaken?'

Rob nodded.

'Do you know what you are supposed to do with such a phrase?'

'That's why I asked to see you. I thought you might know?'

The man muttered the phrase again and then shook his head. 'You'll have to leave that one with me Rob. I have no idea. What site was it on?'

'Oh ... er ...can't remember I was just surfing and came across it.'

'Shame. It's a bit like Tam's premise that the thing doesn't come out to play on weekends or when it's cold. Leave it with me.'

Rob was luxuriating in a bathtub filled with hot water and some scented bubbly stuff he'd found in the bathroom cupboard. His eyes were shut, his feet didn't hurt any more and he was drifting somewhere on a terrace in the Canary Islands, when the phone rang.

Hauling himself from the tub he briefly dried his hands with a towel on the rack in front of the radiator and picked up the handset from the floor where he had left it, together with his change of clothing.

'Yeah?' he asked, tiredly.

'Rob! Rob! Can you get into the theatre tonight?'

'Wha...? Who is this?'

'Vauxhall. Rob, unless we do something *tonight*', the academic stressed the word, 'we are in for all hell breaking loose!'

'You do realise that it's New Years Eve?'

'Yes. Yes. That's the point! I have found out about Mem-he-taw and the golem. If we don't do something tonight we won't be able to control it!'

'What do we have to do?'

'Chalk, CO2 and a branding iron.'

'Eh?' Rob was still not quite with it having wallowed in the warm luxury of the tub for over half an hour.

The Professor continued to issue instructions for the next five minutes about what was to happen – halfway through Rob shivered and pulled a towel around his chilling torso.

Finally, 'Okay. Leave it with me. I'll ring the boys and get as many as I can. See you at the dock door in an hour.'

'Is there any chance of making it sooner?' the academic urged.

'Doubt it. If I know the lads they're probably half pissed by now and taxis will be as scarce as rocking horse shit.'

Billy Marchant and his boss, Barry, had done all the final checks for the on-bridge pyrotechnic display from their mobile headquarters on the Quayside. Fireworks would go off at exactly midnight. They knew it would be exactly at midnight because the computer that controlled the firing sequence was hooked into the time-clock at Greenwich. As soon as that struck twelve the sky would light up.

All the indicator lights on the display appeared to be green.

Rob dialled and a phone rang: 'Tam. What you doing?'

'Jist aboot t' have a can. Why?'

'Sober?'

'Like ah said, first can o' th' night.'

'Theatre. One hour, Urgent.' He disconnected the call before the Scot had any time for questions.

Further calls to Dickie, Harley, Stevie and Foz were all promptly answered and they were all up for doing something to relieve the boredom of the New Year's arrival.

'Me missus has gone to bed,' Stevie replied when asked what his plans were, 'the kids are all at their effin mates' houses and the only thing on the effin telly, apart from effin repeats, is the effin equivalent of the Jimmy effin Shand Band or a crap old effin movie.'

It was only Foz who had a problem.

'I'm twenty miles away – seeing the kid. There's no transport in from here in the sticks.'

Rob thought for a moment before saying, 'I'll get Harley to pick you up.'

The street was almost deserted when Rob's cab pulled up outside the theatre and it cost him almost twenty pounds for the privilege of using the vehicle for a six mile ride.

As he was paying the driver another cab pulled up behind and as he stepped out onto the pavement he could hear Tam's protestations at the exorbitant fee that the driver wanted.

'Ah jist wanted t' ride in the feckin' thing no' bliddy buy i'.' But he passed the notes across anyway.

Dickie followed Tam from the cab with a wry grin on his face.

Since the Bodger was in darkness, due to the fact that the staff always had New Years eve off, the three of them waited under the theatre's awning from the freezing wind, until a bicycle bell alerted them to the fact that Stevie was arriving on two wheels rather than four. Moments later, Harley's motorcycle pulled into the kerb with Foz on the pillion.

They made their way round to the rear of the building. Professor Vauxhall, wearing a heavy brown overcoat and stamping his feet against the cold, was waiting in the shadow of a streetlight.

He greeted them solemnly: 'We don't have long and we have preparations to make before we can confront the golem.'

Rob let them into the theatre using the pass key that he'd used previously with Lil.

They were soon in the crew room and a blow heater was turned on to take the chill from the room; the kettle followed closely.

Once all were seated, with steaming mugs of tea or coffee, the academic opened his briefcase and withdrew a sheaf of notes which he riffled into order.

'Okay Prof, you've got our attention,' Rob stated before sipping a mouthful of tea.

'First, I'm sorry to disrupt any festivities that you may have had planned,' he apologised.

Dickie snorted and shook his head.

Stevie said, 'I can do without a twenty effin first century equivalent of the White effin Heather Club any effin day.'

Tam just grinned and added to the responses with, 'Niver did like Hogmanay. Ah go t' m' relatives in Spain in March f' th' Fallas. Makes Sauchiehall Street on a Sat'day night look like a vicar's tea party.'

Harley grinned. 'Bunch of miserable bastards ain't we?' He had been preparing to have an early night so that he could be up before first light to go on a "run" with a score of other bikers.

The Professor gave a slight smile and referred to his notes. 'The mem-he-taw is a series of three symbols that predate the Hebrew by some considerable time.

'Since our last meeting I've worked almost non-stop to discover what we are up against, by contacting other academics in the field. Finally someone came through from the University in Luxor with exactly the correct solution.

'What we have on the roof is indeed a golem, and when Flynn said the ancient phrase it did indeed bring the thing under his control. This we already knew.

'What we did not know is that if the activator of the golem is killed then the thing believes it has been set free and can, on a certain date, activate other golem to follow its command.' He let this last piece of information sink in before continuing. 'The date that this can happen is today. Midnight.'

'But the golem can't speak, as far as we know,' Dickie stated, 'so how will it activate the other one?'

'Simply by writing "he-mem-he-taw" on it,' Vauxhall replied.

'Just like the Jewish way,' Rob added, nodding.

The Professor shuffled his notes and continued. 'The contact in Luxor has also told me that we need to brand the thing so as to render it totally immobile. It would seem that Stevie's tee-shirt was indeed part of the reason why he is still with us.'

'y' mean that effin Ankh did help?'

The man nodded. 'I wondered how we could brand something that is… semi-stone – other than by employing a mason – and I came up with something I hope will work.' He reached into his briefcase and withdrew a cylindrical object.

'A gas powered soldering iron?' noted Harvey.

'I've adapted it slightly.' The Professor held up the tool so as to show the working end. 'You'll note that I am holding this so that the loop of the Ankh is on the bottom. We need to brand the creature this way up.'

'So the sun is below the horizon,' Dickie informed them.

'Exactly,' confirmed the academic.

'You mentioned CO2 when you were on the phone,' interrupted Rob, 'what's that for?'

'Tam's observation that the golem never bothered the Panto on Saturdays or when it was cold has a ring of truth about it.

'Saturday is still part of the middle-eastern Sabbath, so no work goes on – Sunday being the first day of the working week – and, as the stones are from a somewhat temperate climate, I came to the conclusion that, quite simply, our golem doesn't like the cold.'

The Scot grinned, pleased that he'd been proved right.

'Y' can knit it a effin jumper,' Stevie muttered, as an aside to Tam.

'The theatre won't have any C02, though.' observed Rob, 'They don't keep a stock of it unless they're using dry ice. There's none in this production – we use smoke machines.'

'Ah, but you do have fire extinguishers for the electrics and so forth,' the Professor answered, '*they* will do it.'

For the next half an hour they discussed how they were going to tackle the golem.

'Check that display again will you, Billy?' asked the pyrotechnic boss. 'The flipping thing keeps saying that one of the firing relays is working and then it isn't.'

Billy had been on the Quayside for a break and to soak up some of the atmosphere of the pre-celebration celebrations and had just entered the vehicle with two steaming hot dogs.

'Looks alright to me Boss,' he replied, glancing at the monitor and handing one of the wrapped dogs to Barry.

'I hope so. If that one's dodgy we'll have it either not go off or it'll corrupt the firing sequence.'

'You don't want me to go and look at it do you?'

'Nah. With only forty-six minutes to go I'm not having you crawling girders in the dark.'

'I may not be able to come the whole way with you, Rob,' the Professor confided as the door to the hemp fly floor, above the prompt side of the stage, was opened by Stevie. 'I get somewhat … nervous… when I'm at heights.'

'No bother. Just come as far as you can. We're going along here to the crossover of the proscenium arch where there's a ladder to the grid and the room above the auditorium dome. From there, as I said before, we'll have to go out onto the roof and use the fire escape to get to the front of the building.'

'Ah. Yes. That's the bit. You said that the fire escape is on the edge of the building?'

Rob nodded.

'Hmm…'

'Don't worry. Just come as far as you can and if you're not okay you can stay in the room. Mind the loose rope ends as we go over here.'

With Stevie leading the way they crossed the fly floor gantry to the three steps that led to the crossover and, in near darkness, to the narrow ladder that led upwards to the grid.

Rob turned on his MagLite to show the academic the way.

At the top of the ladder there was a small landing and to the right was the world of pulleys, wires and ropes that ran across the whole grid system to the flying bars below it. The place was dominated by a "Chinaman", a huge cartwheel-type barrel for operating some of the Victorian flying effects for which the venue had been well known in times past. To the left was a narrow door that led into the roof space above the dome which also held the winch machinery for the opulent chandelier that dominated the auditorium.

The room itself was actually a large platform with hand rails at its edges and narrow walkways leading to small louvered doors that led out onto a metal fire escape that ran around the roof of the building and eventually to ground level.

Stevie and the rest of the crew were already through the doors and out onto the roof when the Professor stopped mid-stride at the edge of a walkway.

'You alright Professor?'

'Er…' the man was sweating profusely.

'Acrophobia kicked in?'

The academic nodded his head almost violently.

'Right. Come on we'll get you back down to a safe level.'

'I… I'll… I'll be alright. You need to go to the… the roof.'

'I'll see you to the fly floor,' Rob assured.

Having deposited the academic back on the dressing rooms landing, Rob was retracing his steps and making his way back towards the roof when three shapes appeared, and almost solidified, on the grid.

'*Good luck, Mister Crowther,*' said the first.

Rob turned to look. It was the ghost known as Her Ladyship, accompanied by Jacob Royz and Lil.

'*Shalom, Rob,*' said the old Jew.

'*Good luck, Robert,*' said his old friend, '*And… Happy New Year.*'

They promptly vanished.

'Ten minutes, boss,' stated Billy, slightly louder than normal speech. Barry probably wasn't asleep but "just resting".

'Uh-huh,' he replied opening half an eye, 'tell me at the two.' The eye closed.

Outside, the crowds had grown until the whole of the Quayside next to the bridge was overflowing. The stilt walkers, fire-eaters, clowns and other entertainment had retired five minutes ago and now a local radio DJ had stepped up to the microphone to welcome the dignitaries and the TV soap star that was to press the "big red button" that would launch the first volley of fireworks to welcome in the New Year.

By the time Rob had got back to the dome room and found his way out onto the roof it was blisteringly cold and the wind was starting to blow more than a little. He negotiated the icy cold steel fire escape to the front of the building, where the rest of the crew had been busy.

A rope line had been tied to one of the ornamental urns at the right of the building and fed across the apex, where the urn that was supported by the two statues stood, and tied off to another urn to the left. It had been decided that the only way to get close enough to the statue was to climb out onto the ledge below it so that Rob could chalk the necessary word on its forehead.

Tam and Harley were standing behind the immobile creature with fire extinguishers at the ready and Foz was standing by with the branding iron.

Stevie and Dickie tested the rope's security as Rob dropped down the steel rung ladder to join them.

'Where's the Prof?' Dickie asked, looking around to Rob and giving a final tug at the rope.

'Doesn't like heights.'

'Y' remember whit t' write, eh?' the Scot asked.

'Couldn't really forget could I? Me having been married and split twice. Bloody ironic that the Phoenician for "end it" should be "my ex".'

Earlier in the crew room there had been some hilarity as Vauxhall had shown Rob how to write the symbols to inscribe on the golem. He had taken his pad and a pencil and scribed: "myEx".

'Aye, but dinnae forget the E is backward,' Tam reminded him.

Rob stripped off his blouson to reveal the full body harness over his jeans and sweatshirt, into which he had climbed earlier.

He pulled at the linking strap and checked the karabiner gate was working, then shuddered as the icy wind bit at him before patting his pocket to ensure that the piece of chalk that he was to use was still with him.

Stepping up to the parapet he looked over to the street sixty-odd feet below and then to the narrow ledge that he would have to inch along to get to the statue.

'Alright, Rob?' Dickie asked.

'Ready and willing, Mate. Come on, let's do this.' With that he clipped himself onto the rope with the karabiner and hoisted himself to sit on the ledge.

Stevie came up to him just before he let himself gingerly onto the ledge.

'Don't want to be a effin party pooper but here…' he held up another length of rope, '… safety line.'

Rob nodded and quickly tied the hemp, with a bowline, to a loop on his harness and let himself over the masonry to the narrow ledge six feet below. He tested his footing, gingerly.

He remembered that some twenty-odd years ago the whole frontage of the building had been cleaned and brought back to its Victorian finish. It felt like in the interim that the local pigeon population had been busy. The ledge was inches deep in shit.

'Boss?'

'Yeah, Billy. Two is it?' Barry opened both eyes and rubbed the faux sleep from them.

The man nodded.

'Okay let's make ready. All the signals green?'

Billy checked the monitor. All green on the continuity test so he nodded assent.

Barry rose from his swivel chair and took up his position next to Billy beside the firing consol monitor. All they had to do was use the traffic light system to let the podium know that the five second countdown was about to begin. Currently the signal was at red. At six seconds they would get the amber and at one second the box on the temporary stage would flash green for 'go'.

TV star presses dummy button and the sky lights up. Simple.

As Rob inched his way along the ledge, toeing guano before him, he checked that he would be able to reach the statue's head by occasionally reaching up for distance. No problem; plenty of room.

He was now balanced immediately in front of the colossus and had a moment of slight panic as he thought that the body harness was going to restrict access to his pocket. He fumbled into the pocket and passed the almost restrictive leg strap to feel the piece of chalk. Gripping it between two fingers he carefully withdrew it and then clutched at it. He had not realised how cold his hands had become in the icy weather and so took a moment to breath on them.

'Give it the amber please, Billy,' requested Barry, staring at the clock.

On the podium a little further along the quay the dignitaries and the TV star broke into smiles and the DJ started the countdown…

'Five!'

The crowd responded: 'Four!…' they chorused.

'Boss!' Billy exclaimed, 'We just got a red!'

Three!…

Two!…'

JANUARY

Just as Rob was reaching up to write the Phoenician word, the sky above and to his left exploded in a shower of erupting silver, blue, green and red followed immediately by the most enormous explosions he had ever heard. He dropped the chalk.

'Shit!'

'What the fuck!' came the chorus from above him from the rest of the crew.

Directly in front of him the statue's eyes brightened to a vicious red.

'Double shit!' he cried as he slipped off the ledge and the rope tied to the right urn pulled it from its mounting to send it crashing through the glass awning below, to shatter seconds later on the pavement.

The karabiner and Rob started to slide down the face of the building as the rope played out, but he was pulled up with an almighty jerk as the safety line caught his fall and jerked his groin into his throat. Taking a rasping breath he looked up and could see the golem lean over and stare straight at him.

'Triple fucking shit!'

Just as the sound of more fireworks hit the sky, the CO2 extinguishers popped in the air above but the golem dissipated into a cloud of dust to reform in front of Rob as he dangled fifteen feet below the apex.

The creature hovered only feet away from Rob, its stone wings creaking in the night air.

'Y' alright Rob?' Dickie shouted from above.

'Get me the fuck out of here!' he shouted.

The solid golem reached out with a clawed hand to grab the rope that held Rob and flicked a wickedly pointed tongue at him as its eyes grew redder.

'NOW! For fucks sake!' He trusted to Stevie's rope and unclipped the karabiner. The crossing rope swung away from him, taking the golem with it, as he was unceremoniously hauled towards the roof – catching his shoulder on the ledge as he was dragged past it and again on the capping stones of the top ledge.

Hands reached out to grab him as he grunted in pain and dragged him, panting, onto the roof.

'You okay?' Foz asked.

Trying to catch his breath Rob nodded and rubbed his grazed shoulder.

'C'me're y' wee fuckin' beastie!' yelled Tam, fire extinguisher at the ready, as more fireworks lit up the sky. He leaned over the edge of the roof.

Wings flapped behind them on the raised fly tower. The creature landed on the fire escape and stared at them, ominously.

Stevie crouched down beside Rob to check that he was unhurt and to pass him something that he had taken from his pocket: 'Ever known a effin flyman not to have a piece of effin chalk?' he said, as he pressed a replacement into Rob's palm.

The golem was staring alternately at the exploding fireworks in the sky and then at the theatre crew, as if it did not know which was the greater danger.

'Come to Harley,' stated the biker as he hid the fire extinguisher behind his back and motioned with a hand for the creature to attack him. 'Come on y' Persian prat, come and see what I've got for you.'

Instead of leaping at Harley the golem launched itself at Foz, who was lighting the modified soldering iron. The tool had just struck when the creature grappled the stage technician.

As it clutched at Foz and its tongue flicked around his face he dropped the branding tool which rolled towards Rob.

Tam and Harley leapt forward with their extinguishers and let rip with a continuous icy blast of the gas contained in the canisters. The creature seemed to freeze for a moment, at which Stevie grabbed the chalk from Rob's hand, leapt forward and inscribed "myEx" onto its forehead.

Rob, not to be outdone, grabbed the soldering iron.

The creature seemed to be stunned only for seconds as it clung to Foz, but as soon as Stevie had inscribed the word it seemed to go through a form of petrification and lugubriously flapped its way back to its perch.

Rob was immediately on his feet and pressing the iron to its backside.

'That went well,' Billy observed, 'considering the two reds were to go first then the pair of blues and the four-up of silvers and greens closely followed by the waterfall. Bet that rattled some windows.' He added, 'least ways the titanium reports went off okay.'

'Well, as my old boss in the theatre used to say: "shit happens". Happy New Year.'

'Th… th… tha… thanks guys.' stuttered Foz from under a layer of congealed and frozen CO_2.

'Everyone alright?' Rob asked as he got to his feet, clutching his damaged shoulder which was bleeding through his clothing.

There were nods of ascent and Stevie flicked the piece of chalk over the roof into the street. 'Nasty little effin fucker wasn't it?' he stated as an aside.

'Hopefully that's the last of it,' Dickie sighed as he brushed himself down.

'Only the Professor can tell us that.' Rob struggled to hold back a groan as he began to feel the post-adrenalin pain in his shoulder. He was sure that it was dislocated.

'Crew room?' Stevie asked.

'Over th' roof?' this from Tam.

'Effin Bollix!' Stevie approached the small door on the roof that led back into the theatre and with a deft kick smashed it open. 'They can send me the effin bill.'

'Do we drown our sorrows or celebrate?' Professor Vauxhall asked, as the techies entered the crew room, wet and cold but slightly elated. He held up two bottles of champagne.

'Depends on whether what we've done is enough' Rob stated as he stripped off the harness and layers of clothing to reveal a nasty looking gash on his shoulder.

'You scribed on its forehead and branded it?'

Everyone nodded and Foz added, 'It was touch and go.'

The Professor smiled. 'Then, gentlemen, I would think that all your troubles are over.' He raised the bottles again. 'Shall we?'

They grabbed mugs from the shelf above the sink, the champagne corks popped, and elated toasts were raised.

'Pity Noodles can't be here,' Dickie commented, when the bottles were empty.

Rob, now with his shoulder patched up with the contents of the first aid box, nodded his agreement. 'Well, if the mountain won't come to Mohammed then…?' he grinned.

'Y' cannae go visitin' a hospital at this time o' th' mornin',' Tam stated, looking at his watch, 'its two ay-em.'

'Yes. I don't think the staff would appreciate a… ahem… rather scruffy… bunch of you turning up at this time,' Vauxhall agreed.

'Had your breakfast yet?' Rob asked, as he poked his head around the door to Noodles' room at nine o'clock and smiled.

'If you can count a double dose of morphine as breakfast, yes.' He smiled back, his face wan and drained. He was propped up on several pillows and his right leg, plastered and suspended, was supported on a plastic stand.

'Like I said, if you'd been pissed it wouldn't have happened.' Rob pulled up a chair to the bedside and sat down. 'How did it happen?'

'Tripped over the bloody cat.'

'The cat?' Rob grunted holding back the impulse to laugh. 'Always said you would be brought down by pussy. That'll teach you about getting your leg over.'

'Har. Har. It only hurts when I laugh,' responded a poker-faced Noodles. 'How goes it with our mate on the roof?'

'All sorted. Me and the boys, and the Prof, got the little bugger last night. The Prof says we're safe and sound.'

'Who else got hurt apart from you?' Noodles nodded at the neckline of Rob's tee-shirt from where the edge of medical gauze and sticking plaster protruded.

'Just a scratch, Mate. Foz got a bit iced up but apart from that everyone's okay.'

'Tell them hello from me.'

'Will do. Some of them will be along in the next couple of days. How long you going to be in here?'

Noodles shrugged. 'This pot on my leg's going to be there for a while and then they're going to see if I need more pinning back together.'

'You going to be okay for money?'

'Insurance up to the eyeballs. No worries,' Noodles replied, nodding

'That's a shame.'

'Oh?'

'Yeah.' Rob reached into his blouson and pulled out a stuffed envelope. 'You'll not be needing this.' With a grin he threw the open packet onto the sheets where it spilled out a bundle of currency. 'We had a whip-round.'

'Flipping heck!' Noodles fingered some of the notes, 'Who..?'

'Cast, crew, front of house. Just about everyone.' Rob winked, 'Oh, and Tom says if you're prostrate for a while he'll come over and "give you a hand".'

'Tell him thanks but no thanks. I've got that sorted.'

'Twirlie?' grinned Rob.

'Might be?' Noodles grinned back.

'I'd better get to work. Anything else you need?'

'Hip flask of malt would be good. This morphine is self administered and sometimes it's not enough, y'know.'

'Okay, I'll sort that.'

'Hang on. You're going to work? There's no show today.'

'Yeah, I know. But a part of the Prince of Denmark just won't let go of me.' Rob stood and had the door open before Noodles could respond. Just before the door closed Rob stuck his head back around it and said: 'Oh, and Happy New Year.'

EPILOGUE

Noodles, Tam and Dickie were all sitting at the usual table in The Bodger, each of them nursing a pint.

'He did say one o'clock?' asked Noodles, glancing at the reflection of the clock over the bar in the mirror, which read a minute to.

Heads nodded.

'What the hell is all this about?' said Dickie before taking a mouthful of beer.

'Beats me.' replied Tam, 'Ah wis just aboot t' make mesel' a bacon sarnie when the phone rang.' He eyed the bar menu with some thought.

'What can be so urgent that a solicitor wants to see us on Easter Sunday?'

'Nae doubt we're aboot t' find oot,' nodded Tam towards a slightly balding man in a brown overcoat who was approaching the bar, carrying a Gladstone-style bag.

The barmaid pointed directly at the company.

'Gentlemen, my name is Smith, solicitor.' He placed a business card on the table, 'May I join you?'

'Pint?' asked Dickie.

'Not at present. I may after we have concluded our business.' With that he dragged a carver chair from the adjoining table and sat down, placing his bag on the floor.

He paused.

'My client has instructed me to give you certain items, and once you have carried out the instructions then I am to give you a further item.'

'An' who's y' client?'

'I am not at liberty to say.'

'"Certain items"' observed Dickie, 'not a summons or...' he left the words unsaid.

'I can assure you that what we, you, are about to do is advantageous.' With that he drew the bag up from the floor and onto his lap, opened it and placed a toy Aladdin's lamp on the table beside a pad and pencil.

'My client instructs me to ask you rub the lamp and to make a wish.'

Noodles looked the solicitor straight in the eye. 'You are joking?'

'Very far from a joke. This is just the first part of two instructions.'

'Aye. An' next y'll want us tae run bullock naked through town.'

'I assure you Mister…'

'Tam,' he replied, suspiciously.

'I assure you, Tam, that running through town in the altogether is not involved.'

'Rub it and make a wish?' said Dickie picking up a lamp.

'Out loud,' the solicitor instructed.

Sheepishly the man rubbed the lamp. 'A new car and a holiday.'

The solicitor wrote down the wish.

'Ah fuck it. If ahm on "You've Been Framed"…' Tam took the lamp and rubbed. 'A million quid.'

The solicitor wrote again.

'Hang on a mo',' paused Noodles, 'I take it from the lamp that this has something to do with the panto. If so, why aren't Rob, Stevie and Harley here?'

'Stevie I saw at work not half an hour ago. Harley I saw in hospital; he has, unfortunately, had a slight spill from his motorcycle. Mister Crowther is in the south, so one of our other representatives is dealing with that.'

Noodles nodded: 'I'm with Tam.' He looked around for hidden cameras and then rubbed his lamp. 'Get this damn leg fixed privately. The NHS has crap waiting times.'

'Thank you, Gentlemen.' The lawyer returned the lamp, paper

and pencil to his bag, withdrew a brown Manila envelope and from that took three smaller envelopes. He laid them carefully around the table with the instruction that they were not to open them until he had left.

With that he stood up, returned the carver to its original position then turned and left the pub.

'It's a joke, right?' this from Dickie as he stared at an envelope with his name on it.

'Only one way to find out.' Noodles ripped the edge of the envelope and withdrew a folded card wallet. Opening it he just stared at its contents.

'Weel?'

'Open yours.'

Tam and Dickie simultaneously opened theirs and withdrew a similar wallet.

'Fuck!'

'Nah!'

'Canary Islands?'

They both turned over the tickets that were held within the folder.

'You got one of these as well?' asked Noodles, holding up a slip of paper that read: "Pick-up is Techies".'

'Yup!' they chorused.

Two days, and about two and a half thousand miles later, Noodles, Dickie and Tam disembarked at the "Aeropuerto De Gran Canaria" by-passing luggage collection – they only carried hand luggage – and after passport checks made their way to the front of the terminal building that was buzzing with tourists and holiday reps.

They scanned the crowded doorways for their pick-up sign.

It was Tam that noticed a piece of cardboard scrawled with the word "Tekkys" held high by a small olive skinned man wearing sunglasses, white shirt and black pants.

'You picking up the techies?' asked Noodles.

'Si, senor,' he nodded, 'Tan, Dick an' Noodle?'

'Aye. That's us.'

'Follow, por favour. I am Paulo. I have car waiting.' and with that he darted to the automatic door of the airport and led them across the bus transfer street to a waiting stretch Mercedes with smoked windows.

As he held open the rear door he asked, 'I take your bag, yes?'

The three men, somewhat stupefied by their greeting, handed their luggage to the driver and got into the air conditioned vehicle.

They set off at great speed once the driver was behind the wheel and with much hooting of the car-horn.

'Whit the fuck is all this aboot?' asked Tam over the driver's shoulder.

'Senor?'

'This. This... car. The flights?' joined Dickie.

'No comprede, senor. I take you to villa in Tauro. About forty minutes.' and with that raised the glass divider between driver and passenger compartment.

'Guess we'll just have to enjoy the view, boys.' suggested Noodles. 'Our benefactor is only forty minutes away.'

The final destination announced itself as a chalet-style villa set in stunning surroundings from which one could see the azure blue ocean to one side and mountain views to the other.

Pablo opened the rear door to let the three men out.

Smith, the solicitor, now dressed in a light business suit, was waiting for them on the top of a set of marble tiled steps at the entrance to the villa.

'Good afternoon, Gentlemen. Would you please follow me?'

He led the way through the spacious villa to a set of sliding French doors and out onto a patio that held a large figure of eight swimming pool, several recliners and a table and chairs shadowed by a large sun umbrella. He then returned into the villa.

Stevie was lying on a recliner wearing only a pair of bright blue shorts and holding a can of sweating Dorada beer to his forehead.

'About effin time. Where you been?' he grinned. 'Pull up a effin beer.'

'Afternoon boys. Welcome to my small place in the Canaries,' said Rob's voice from behind them.

'Rob! What the hell is going on? You won the Lotto or something?' asked Dickie, turning.

'Or something. Come on sit down. I'll explain.'

Rob walked to the shaded table and placed on it a six-pack of chilled beers and a yellow folder.

Once the four of them were seated, and beers passed around, he started.

'Remember when we chased the golem to its final place and we did all that hokus-pokus and the stuff with the Ankh?'

All heads nodded.

'Well, just as the little twat sat down and turned back to stone I saw something glint under its backside. I snuck back, the next day, to see what it was.'

'And..?' came the chorus.

'Well, once I'd got the coping stone off – and the stonework – I had to wrench the statue from its base. Guess what I found?'

'A diamond necklace?' said Dickie.

Tam suggested a gold bar.

'Nope. I found out why it was called Goldenstern. A coin.'

'A coin?' repeated Noodles.

'Yup. An Edward the Third Double Leopard.'

'So?' Tam was curious.

'A bit of history, which you all know, is that the theatre was opened in eighteen sixty-seven. Some years before that – about 1857

– it's believed that two coins, were dredged up from the River Tyne. Edward the Third Double Leopards. Britain's first gold coin.'

'And...?' enquired Noodles, popping the ring-pull on his tin.

'And they ended up in the British Museum. A third coin was dug up in 2005 or six and was auctioned for a fair bit of money. The one I found was what they call FDC, Mint Condition.'

'How much is a fair bit?' Tam was now stripping off his shirt.

'Four hundred and sixty thousand pounds.' Rob lifted the lid on a box of coronas, snipped the end off the cigar and lit it from his lighter. 'Nothing to say?' he grinned.

'Y' mean…' Tam waved his arm at the surroundings.

'Ah, no. This is just rented for the month.'

'What happened to the coin you found Rob?' asked Noodles, 'Auction?'

'Uh-huh,' he breathed out a cloud of cigar smoke, 'to a Yank. And I'm going to share the proceeds with you boys,' he smiled. 'Call it retirement.' He pulled from the folder a slip of paper and raised his voice towards the house. 'Mister Smith. If you would be so kind, please.'

The solicitor appeared carrying three briefcases and placed them next to Rob on the ground.

Rob picked up the first case. 'Tam. It's not a million quid, Mate, but I'm sure you'll like what it is.' He passed the case across to the Scotsman.

'Dickie. You got your holiday. I think you should be able to afford a car.'

'Noodles. Get your leg fixed.' He passed the other two cases across the table.

There was a short pause before three sets of locks were snapped open, but the lids of the cases remained closed in anticipation.

'How mu…?' squeaked Noodles.

'Well, after expenses the divvie up between the five of us is…' and then he mumbled through a plume of smoke.

'What?' shouted the chorus.

Stevie, still beside the pool, grinned and shouted, 'Three-hundred and four thousand effin quid!'

Rob grinned, 'Cigar anyone?'

Also Available by Slim Palmer

The Albert Tales

Three illustrated short stories:

Albert and the Golden Quaver : Albert and the Dragons Egg

Albert and the Christmas Elf

240 pages :: Illustrated :: ISBN: 1905363354

Albert Tales Too

Three illustrated short stories:

Albert and the Fairies : Albert and the Haggis

Albert and the Wizard

240 pages :: Illustrated :: ISBN: 1905363842

Albert The Third

Three illustrated short stories:

Albert and the Witches : Albert and the Time Machine

Albert and the Gargoyles

240 pages :: Illustrated :: ISBN: 1846851157

Kryptos - An Albert Tale

A full length story where Albert is asked by Mister Bufoe, Granny Poad's
Dwarven gardener - and sometimes toad - to help recover items that
will restore an Oracle.

252 pages :: Illustrated :: ISBN: 9781846853845

Skriveners - The Second Book of Kryptos

The follow-up to Kryptos in which Albert and company have to help
defeat the Elk Herder Dwarven terrorist cell and are faced with a semi-
retired Demon and his assistant.

256 pages :: Illustrated :: ISBN: 9781846858925

What people are saying about the Alberts...

THE ALBERT TALES:

***** 5 Stars - Very readable ... Highly recommended.

Ideal for reading to children of ages seven and up...
... older children and adults will also enjoy it.

ALBERT TALES TOO:

***** 5 Stars - ... full marks for content, drawing and imagination.

***** 5 Stars - If you want a good read for your kids buy the 'Alberts'.

ALBERT THE THIRD:

***** 5 Stars - ... may have been written for children/teens but as an adult it was easy to slip into Albert's world ... brilliant!

There is something appealing about Albert... the whole package would be great for reading aloud at bedtime.

KRYPTOS:

***** 5 Stars - Fast paced and hugely entertaining...

Slim Palmer, who wrote his first 'theatre' novel, "Operation Brutus", under the pen name of Stiofán McAtinney - as he thought it wise at the time as they are more adult novels and not to be confused with his 'Albert' series of books, worked in theatre for over fifteen years and put shows into many venues across Britain including London's West End.

He lives in an anomaly of Northumberland.

www.slimpalmer.com

Printed in the United Kingdom by
Lightning Source UK Ltd., Milton Keynes
137756UK00001B/187-195/P